☑ P9-AQO-508

vibes

Y ... GOD HER NOSE IS STUBBY! LOOK HOW HER ARMS JIGGLE!
'T CARE WHAT HER DAD DID, THERE'S NO EXCUSE ... NOT TH
N. WHY CAN'T E U C AT ... I MAY

vibes

L MAKE THE O O OU S SICK ... W
S SHE WEAR THOSE HORRIBLE OUTFITS? WHAT A BITCH! SHE'S G
H FAT ANKLES! SHE PROBABLY SMELLS ... HER HAIR IS SO UG

Written by
Amy Kathleen Ryan

Houghton Mifflin Company

Boston ✦ 2008

www.houghtonmifflinbooks.com

The text of this book is set in Dante.

Library of Congress Cataloging-in-Publication Data
Ryan, Amy Kathleen.
Vibes / written by Amy Kathleen Ryan.
p. cm.
Summary: Kristi, a sophomore in an alternative high school, thinks that
nearly everyone dislikes her but begins to doubt her psychic insights after
learning long-held family secrets and some classmates' true feelings.
ISBN 978-0-618-99530-1
[1. Self-perception—Fiction. 2. Interpersonal relations—Fiction.
3. Psychic ability—Fiction. 4. High schools—Fiction. 5. Schools—Fiction.
6. Family problems—Fiction.] I. Title.
PZ7.R9476Vib 2008
[Fic]—dc22
2008001865

Manufactured in the United States of America

MP 10 9 8 7 6 5 4 3 2 1

✦

FOR RICHARD,
WHO HAS MADE IT POSSIBLE
FOR ME TO WRITE
WITH AUTHORITY ABOUT
TRUE LOVE

✦

PSYCHIC

It isn't easy being able to read minds. People think up some pretty nasty sewage. Like the other day—I'm walking home from school when I come across an old guy walking his smelly Doberman. He's definitely a candidate for this year's Stodgiest American Award. Black suit coat, gray pants, white stuff in the corners of his mouth. He takes one look at my thick legs in their fishnets and my skirt that I made out of Mylar birthday balloons and my tank top that barely contains my ginormous boobs and finally the eyeliner I cake over my eyes because it makes me look dangerous, and he thinks: *Ugly bitch.*

Well, it's true. I'm a bitch. And I'm ugly.

I could shed a lot of light on human nature if people knew that I read minds. Scientists would study me. I'd be in some lab strapped to a table and they'd put a huge machine around my head to measure my brain waves, and they'd nod to one another and say, "Fascinating. Fascinating." And they'd all have really big pores and very white skin, because scientists never go outside. That's why I don't talk to anyone except for my Aunt Ann about my powers. The last thing I need is re-searchers sticking needles into my brain.

If you're wishing you were psychic, too, believe me, you do *not* want to know what people are thinking. People are mean, nasty, selfish slobs, and 99 percent of the time their brain vibes hurt your feelings and you have to go around trying not to remember that Gusty Peterson, the cutest guy in school, looked at you yesterday and thought, *Sick*.

I don't like Gusty Peterson anyway. He always wears base-ball caps backwards and extra-big jeans, and he tries to walk with a loose, tough-guy swagger that makes him look dumb. He's a jerk-off. Too bad he also happens to be so gorgeous that when you look at his perfect tanned face and blond curls your eyes water.

That's one more thing I can tell you about human nature: beautiful people are the last ones you want to befriend. Beautiful people float through life thinking that it's perfectly natural for others to gaze at them adoringly, and open doors for them, and defer to their opinion about whether or not the streamers for the prom should droop in the middle. Doesn't anyone understand that beautiful people are stupid? That's why nature made them beautiful, so they'd have some chance of surviving in the wild. And how do they survive? They use people and then they drop people, and they float away on the currents of their own gorgeousness to the next poor girl who thinks that being friends with a beautiful person will some-how make her beautiful, too. I've got news for you: Hanging around beautiful people just makes you uglier by comparison.

I learned all this from my ex–best friend, Hildie Peterson—Gusty's sister. She is one of the most gorgeous people in the whole world. She's skinny and petite. Her eyes are slanty like a cat's and her hair is light blond and glossy, so when you first see it you think that color can't be natural, but then when you get closer you realize that it's totally natural and you feel even worse about your mousy brown. She has never had a pimple in her entire life, and she's been doing gymnastics since she was four years old, so she glides like a swan. She's practically a freak, she's so beautiful.

I used to like her, when she didn't understand how pretty she was. That was until we hit high school and suddenly the entire lacrosse team was asking her out. They loved her so much, they practically carried her on their shoulders through the hallways of the school. Did Hildie ever look back at me—her big-breasted, psychic, slightly freaky friend—as she drifted into the stratosphere of popularity?

Would you?

MORNING

Alarm clocks were invented by fork-tongued devils disguised as gremlins wearing snake masks. Today when my alarm goes off I nearly get whiplash, it scares me so much.

I roll out of bed. I can *literally* roll out of bed because I keep my laundry piled on the floor right next to my mattress. It's like my exit ramp. Today I execute the move perfectly, and I end up on my back next to my dresser. Right above my head Minnie Mouse is curled up in my open sock drawer. I have so many special socks I can't close it, which is fine because it's Minnie's favorite perch. All my socks are covered in hair, but I don't mind. It's part of my look. Minnie looks down at me and purrs.

I adore my cat. The only thing she ever thinks about me is "I love you. I love you. I love you." She's thinking it now as she crinkles her pretty yellow eyes at me. "Hi, Minnie," I whisper, and she purrs even louder.

Minnie Mouse never meows. This is very lucky, because if my mom ever found Minnie, the cause of her constant allergies would be obvious. Then I might have to fight an epic battle against the forces of evil, a.k.a. my mother, to keep Minnie. I would never let her go. Minnie is my best friend and my secret furry weapon all rolled into one. Who could give up that combination?

Hiding Minnie all this time has been a challenge, but it helps that Mom works sixty hours a week. Plus, when I first got Minnie, I gave Mom this whole elaborate speech about how I was suffocating and I needed her to respect my boundaries by not coming into my room. Once I got her to promise she'd never trespass again, I installed a padlock with only one key, which I keep on a chain around my neck at all times. Mom hated the lock, and it caused the worst mother-daughter war of all time, but I finally won because I'm younger, I have more energy, and I could hold out longer. Now my domain and my cat are protected.

I pull Minnie down from her perch and snuggle her in my pile of laundry before I finally get on my feet and stumble into my bathroom. Because my mom is a surgeon, we have a really nice house, so my bedroom has its own adjoining bathroom, which is my favorite place in the whole world.

I slide into my huge pink bathtub and wait for the water to slowly edge over my legs and up my belly, until it finally makes my ginormous boobs float. I sit in the hot water trying to psych myself up for the day. I have a mantra: *I am my own person. I am my own person. I am my own person.*

That's why I don't have many friends.

I check my fingers for pruniness. I like to wait in the tub until my hands are so waterlogged they're practically white. Then I slip into my chenille bathrobe and sit in front of my vanity mirror to begin the makeup procedure: eyeliner, eye shadow, eyeliner, mascara, eyeliner, lipstick, and maybe eyeliner. I cannot upset the order in which I apply my makeup because otherwise I just don't look right.

Once I'm made up, I go to my "found" wardrobe. I call it "found" for a reason. Last year in Self-Expressions and Language Arts class, Betty Pasternak, the only semicool teacher I've ever had, taught us about found poetry. You cut out words and phrases from magazines and make poems from them. I used clips from the playmate profile in *Playboy*. Betty said my poem was subversive. That is my favorite word. *Subversive.*

Anyway, when Betty explained found poetry, I realized that's what my wardrobe is. I never buy material for my sewing; I find it — at the Salvation Army, in my mom's closet, even in dumpsters and abandoned buildings. Today I put on my potato-sack peasant skirt with my extra-thick petticoat so I don't itch and my black tunic that I made from the fabric of ripped-up umbrellas I found on the street after a bad rainstorm.

I look mahvelous — as mahvelous as possible for someone with watermelon-size gazungas.

Now it's time to venture out. I creep out of my room and, as I quietly lock the padlock on my door, listen carefully for signs of Mom. The house is quiet, which probably means

Mom is already at the hospital, or maybe she never got home last night. Still, it pays to be cautious.

Slowly, so that the zippers on my purple go-go boots don't rattle, I creep down the plush carpet of our hallway until I can just barely look around the corner into the kitchen. *Please don't be there. Please don't be there.*

She's there.

She's still in her scrubs, boobs sagging, her butt spread out on the stool. No wonder Dad left. She's let her hair grow out like brown weeds, and it's super thick like mine, so she always wears it in a big fat bun on her head. She never wears any makeup, and she's getting to the age where she needs at least a little blush, but I guess she doesn't really care how she looks. She's leaning her elbows on the counter, her face toward the polished granite, a steaming mug of coffee in front of her.

Mom must have worked all night. She has her back to me, and she's so out of it, I just might pull this off.

I slide around the refrigerator to the cabinet and carefully open it just enough to pull out the All-Bran Crunchy Tarts. I watch her for signs of life. She has not moved a muscle.

Now comes the hard part. I fish through my backpack for my travel mug. I haven't washed it in a while, so it's coated with a thick film of old coffee, but it doesn't matter because I drink my coffee black and the residue just adds to the dimension of the flavor. It's my special blend, if you will.

Carefully I slide the coffeepot off the burner and take it into the living room. I smell it to see what beans she used. It's got that slightly metallic, bitter warmth to it that I love.

Colombian. I hold it up to the window, but the coffee seems to absorb all light. My mom is Greek, so she makes our coffee super thick, just the way I like it.

I pour myself a nice big cupful. There's enough to fill my whole travel mug, praise be to the gods. Not that they exist.

I quietly set the decanter on the end table and make a run for it.

"Kristi?" she calls as I open the door.

I close it behind me without answering, but I can hear in her thoughts that she knows I heard.

Why does my daughter hate me so much? That's what she's thinking.

SCHOOL

My walk to school isn't as bad as a perp walk to the courthouse for someone wrongfully accused of strangling her own children, but that's only because there aren't crowds of reporters taking my picture as I approach the institutional building of my doom.

I live in a suburb of a suburb. I'm surrounded by the offspring of professional people who attend parent-teacher meetings and volunteer on Election Day. They believe in a liberal education, and everybody who's anybody sends their kids to the nontraditional hippie-dippie school that offers children and teens a self-directed, cross-disciplinary, nonauthoritarian education in an emotionally safe environment.

It's excruciating.

They don't even call it a school. They call it *Journeys*.

"Hey, Kristi," someone lisps from behind me. Jacob Flax runs to catch up, his eyes on my boobs. I get a flash of myself taking a bubble bath. He always imagines my boobs wet for some reason. Jacob waves over his shoulder at someone. "See you, Felix!"

Felix Mathers waves back. Felix is the cadaverous musical genius who plays nine instruments. He is a weird dude. He and Jacob walk to school together until they hit my block, and then Jacob breaks off to join me and Felix always hurries away.

Today I finally ask Jacob about it. "Why doesn't Felix ever walk with us?"

"He's shy."

"Shy about what?"

"Shy about girls, I guess," Jacob says, glancing at my cleavage.

If reading minds has taught me nothing else, it's that teenage guys are so horny that every moment of their lives is exquisite torture. Jacob is no exception. We'd probably be better friends if he wasn't always picturing my naked torso.

It doesn't help that he spits when he talks.

"What are you wearing today?" He looks me up and down.

"Umbrellas and a potato sack. The umbrellas symbolize the earth's love for her living creatures, and the potatoes represent the response of all living things to the healing waters of the sky." (I only half mean this. I enjoy blowing his mind.)

"Well, you look cool." He stares at his shoes, which have holes. He must have nine pairs of canvas high-tops, and every pair has holes in exactly the same place, right over his big toes. "I'm getting braces."

"That's nice." I take a swig of my coffee. Sweet lifeblood.

"I'm getting the braces you can't see? The invisible ones?" he says, spraying me with saliva.

Good thing I'm wearing umbrellas.

"Maybe braces will act as a splashguard for your mouth," I say as I wipe myself off.

"Sorry. I'm paying for them myself. Dad says the American preoccupation with straight teeth is a waste of money." Jacob's parents are English, but that's not the reason they're weird. They're so pale that when you first see them you think they're dead, and when you get to know them, you wish they were.

"Your parents are preoccupied with 'American preoccupations.'"

"Tell me about it! Anyway, I earned enough at my job at the library over the summer to save up for orthodonture," he spits.

"That's enterprising." We're almost to the school building. I have to drink my coffee fast. As I pour it down my throat, I get a flash of Jacob imagining me drinking coffee under a waterfall in Hawaii. Poor bastard.

"Do you think I'll look better if I get braces?" He grabs my arm and turns me to look at him. He smiles wide, his pale lips framing snaggly teeth. I lean away so I can be objective.

"Yes, but you also need to work out and wash your hair every day," I say.

"Great idea!" he says, as if I just suggested he wear a tuxedo to school.

Suddenly I'm sideswiped by a deeply bitchy vibe: *Why does she wear those horrible outfits?* I don't have to turn because I can see her from the corner of my eye. Eva Kearns-Tate, a.k.a. Evil Incarnate. Without looking at her, I flip her the bird.

"Jesus, Kristi!" screams Eva. "Get a life!"

"What was that for?" Jacob glances timidly at Eva. He fears the wrath of the cool.

Smiling at Eva, I blow on my fingertip before slipping it into an imaginary holster.

Eva huffs and marches up the stairs into the school, her long black hair wagging behind her. It's not fair that the gorgeous get more gorgeous when they're pissed, while the ugly just get more hideous.

"Why are you so mean to Eva?" Jacob asks.

I pretend I don't hear and slip on my headphones. As we walk into the school I turn up Maria Callas as high as I can without risking permanent hearing loss. Opera is the only way to dampen the vibes ricocheting around me. *What a bitch! She's got such fat ankles! She probably smells. Her hair is so ugly. God, her nose is stubby! Look how her arms jiggle! I don't care what her dad did, there's no excuse . . .*

And on and on and on.

Gee, I love high school.

We all head to the activity center, where we form a nonhier-
archical circle. I notice Gusty Peterson talking to Eva. He has
one arm folded over his middle, which makes him look
weirdly insecure. Today he's wearing normal pants and a
green rugby shirt that somehow brings out the gold highlights in his perfectly wavy hair. He murmurs something in
Evil Incarnate's ear, and she giggles. Her dark eyes wander
over the room until they rest on me. Gusty looks at me, too.
His thought sails across the room at me, pinging off people's
words and fears to land right in the cup of my ear: *Sick.*

I look away. This is nothing new. He thinks, *Sick,* every
time he looks at me. I don't care what Gusty Peterson thinks,
anyway. He's a moron.

Everyone except me is talking and laughing while we wait
for Brian to start the meeting. Brian stands off to the side with
the other teachers, his hands tucked under his chin, a big
smile on his face. He's all the way across the room under the
basketball hoop, but I can still see that his teeth are slightly
green. Everything about Brian is *slightly.* He's slightly tall,

slightly fat, slightly smart, and slightly hostile. His eyes are slightly too far apart, and one of them is always looking slightly off to the side, so that all the expressions on his face seem extreme. When he smiles it's like his whole face is splitting with happiness, and when he's mad his face shortens until you have to wonder how his brain isn't getting squished. He's a weird-looking dude, but everyone pretends to revere him, including the parents, because he founded the school. I've even heard people refer to him as a pedagogical genius. I think he's more like one of those traveling professional hypnotists who mesmerizes entire crowds. He talks in a really soothing voice and always holds his hands out in a calming gesture while he smiles his way through a speech about love, common values, and inner peace.

Slowly Brian walks to the center of the circle and smiles at the floor for a while. We're all supposed to quiet down, but everyone keeps talking. It's easy to take advantage of a nonauthoritarian principal. Soon he begins to laugh as if he's absolutely delighted with the way we are enjoying ourselves, but I sense a twinge of frustration beneath his tight smile. Then he starts waving his hands at the floor and walking in a little circle. He looks so freaky, people stop to watch him. The murmuring peters out and everyone focuses.

"Good morning," he cries, as if he were the first person to come up with just the right words to describe a perfect day. He holds out one hand to someone in the crowd. "Mallory, come join me."

A super tall guy wanders over to Brian in the center of the

circle. He looks shaky as he scans the crowd. His hair is neon orange, and it's bushy and very long. He has it crammed into a ponytail, but it looks like any second the rubber band will explode and his hair will escape to roam the earth, staging military coups and taking high-profile hostages. He has the absolute worst acne I've ever seen, and the redness of it vibrates against the orange of his hair so that he's almost difficult to look at. He's quite grotesque. But I like his white jeans and his white T-shirt and his white bomber jacket. He's clearly a reject from some other private school. Journeys is the stopping-off spot for a lot of kids on their way to juvenile detention.

"This is Mallory, everyone, who's come here from the Learning Center. Let's welcome him to our community."

"Welcome, Mallory," everyone drones.

Mallory scratches at his neck just where the pimples are the most swollen. Brian stares at him until Mallory clears his throat and mumbles, "Hi." Then he practically runs for the outer rim of the circle.

Brian smiles kindly at Mallory and then calls to the ceiling in joy: "Does anyone have something special to share?" My ex-friend Hildie Peterson raises her hand, and Brian smiles warmly at her. "Yes, Hildie?"

"I just wanted to say that I noticed the tree at the edge of the schoolyard is blooming." She twinkles her slanty eyes at Brian, who twinkles right back.

"Yes! We're so lucky to have an autumn cherry tree on our campus! I think everyone should make it their business during

Afternoon Personal Time to go and enjoy those gorgeous blooms! See how they smell, stroke them, lie under the tree and notice how the sun dapples your body with light." He stretches out his arms as if the entire universe is giving him a massage. "Let's all thank Hildie for this wonderful reminder of how beautiful our world is!"

I'm not kidding. This is Morning Meeting. This is my daily hell.

"Does anyone else have something to share?" Brian trains his eyes on the crowd. (Well, he trains one eye on us, one at the wall, but I'm pretty sure he's trying to look at us.) Most of us look at the floor, but to my disgust and horror Jacob raises his hand. Brian smiles at Jacob with a mixture of revulsion and pity. "Yes, Jacob?" he coos. "What do you have to share?"

"I've decided on my individual project for this year." Jacob sprays the poor girl standing next to him, but she's too nice to wipe it off right away. "My individual project is me."

"Oh?" Brian asks, raising one eyebrow with delight. I guess he isn't delighted enough to raise both eyebrows.

"Yes!" Jacob says eagerly. His entire skinny body practically vibrates with excitement. "My individual project this year is going to be self-improvement."

Brian claps his hands. "Wonderful! I think it was Aldous Huxley who said, 'There is only one corner of the universe you can be certain of improving, and that is yourself.'" Brian slowly rotates in the middle of our circle so that he can make precious eye contact with each and every one of us. When his eyes meet mine he thinks, *Troublemaker.* "I think we should all be supportive of Jacob's efforts this year! Let's give him a round of applause!"

Everyone claps for Jacob Flax, and a few people start whistling and catcalling, including Gusty Peterson, who shakes his fist while yelling, "Yeah! Yeah!" Evil Incarnate holds up her hands over her head and claps super enthusiastically. I watch Jacob to see if he understands what's happening, but he is blushing and smiling with glee.

He has no idea he is being mocked.

EXPLORATIONS OF NATURE

After Morning Meeting I head to my first class, Explorations of Nature, which is biology in disguise. Every one of our classes is supposed to be interdisciplinary, which is another word for "confusing." Math is called "The Language of the Universe," and English is "Story as Cultural Artifact." I have Maria Callas warbling in my ears, but that doesn't keep me from hearing my ex–best friend, Hildie Peterson, think, *Why does she have to sit so close to me?* when I take the chair behind her. I'm sitting here because it's the only padded chair left, but of course she's so self-centered, she would never think of that.

Our school doesn't have desks in the classrooms because Brian thinks they conceal our inner states and inhibit the free motion of our bodies. I glance at David, who is seated on his teacher stool, staring out the window and stroking his goatee. All the girls think he's totally hot, and they all flirt with him, which is pathetic, but what's even more pathetic is that he flirts right back.

"Hi, David!" Hildie calls, flashing her blond hair at him.

"Hildie," he says in an intimate tone. His black eyes practically rub against her as he smiles.

I don't know *how* he hasn't gotten fired.

Today David has written another Robert Frost poem on the board. The poem says:

> *Then when I was distraught*
> *And could not speak,*
> *Sidelong, full on my cheek,*
> *What should that reckless zephyr fling*
> *But the wild touch of thy dye-dusty wing!*

Either David likes Robert Frost or Frost is the only poet he knows. That's okay, because I actually like him. Frost, not David, who I especially dislike today. On the little table in front of him is a mutilated caterpillar. What used to be a cute, fuzzy, green little wormy animal has become a science exhibit for how gross nature is. Class hasn't begun yet, but I don't care. I raise my hand.

David pretends not to see me. I can hear him thinking, *Oh God, not again.* This does nothing to stop me. I wave my hand in his face. The second his eyes flicker over me, I launch into it: "What right do you have to kill that poor defenseless creature?"

"I didn't," he says wearily. "I found it dead on my lawn." I catch a brief flash of the caterpillar lying helplessly in front of David's Birkenstock sandal, motionless. But I can't tell from the image if it was really a goner yet.

"How did you *know* it was dead?" I hear sniggering behind

me, and a whole wave of thoughts rushes over me. *Not this again. Why can't she shut up? God, her neck is fat.* This only strengthens my resolve. "Maybe it was just stunned."

"It was dead."

"Did you hold a tiny mirror up to its nose to see if it was breathing?"

"Kristi, I can tell when a caterpillar is dead."

"Did you try to resuscitate it?"

"How do you suggest I do that?"

"You could get a tiny straw."

"Surely you're not serious."

I open my mouth to assure him that I am quite serious (I'm not), but he holds his hand up in my face. "So, how is everyone today?" David asks the class at large.

"Better than that caterpillar," Casey Spinelli says in his squeaky voice. Everyone laughs.

Ha ha ha.

David pretends to be amused as he leans over the tiny cadaver. "I found this poor little guy this weekend. He'd frozen the night before. I thought this would be a great opportunity to begin our unit on anatomy."

I look around the room to see if anyone is buying his story about the caterpillar's natural death. Last year, when he tried to show the tenth-graders the internal organs of a frog, Brian stormed into the room, red-faced, and gave David a lecture about the sanctity of all life. David is no longer allowed to use animals in his classes. We can't even have bug collections.

This is the one thing I agree with Brian about. How would you feel if a huge frog drugged you, cut you open, and splayed you on a corkboard so the tadpoles could jab at your liver?

"Crowd around, everyone," David says as he waves us up. We all stand around him while he pokes tweezers around the caterpillar's eensie-weensie internal organs. We trade off with magnifying glasses so everyone can get a big, gross eyeful.

Once David is done with the caterpillar, he hands out a chart of human anatomy. I see what's coming, so I raise my hand and stand right in front of David's face. Whenever I feel partner work coming on, I go to the bathroom so that by the time I come back everyone already has a partner and I can work alone. I practically beg David with my eyebrows, *Please let me go!* But he's onto me, because he thinks, *Not this time, Kristi,* just before he announces, "Everyone find a partner and quiz each other about internal organs."

Time for Plan B: *Initiate isolation sequence.*

I discreetly slip my earphones on. Maria Callas is getting to the first big crescendo when I feel a pressure on my arm. Hildie is standing over me, and when I look at her she rolls her eyes. "Everyone else has a partner. David said I should work with you." This is when I notice that Bella Polokov is not here today, which means that poor Hildie is without her usual ally.

I would rather be consumed by a million caterpillars in an act of misguided revenge than work with my treacherous former best friend, but all I can do is shrug. She sits next to me, crossing one perfectly toned leg over the other. She looks at me uncertainly as she thinks, *I may as well make the best of this.* "Who first?" she says.

"I don't care," I say.

Here we go again with the martyr routine, I hear her thinking. "Okay. Where is the stomach?"

I point to the heart.

"No, Kristi. Where really?"

I point to the brain.

"No!" she says, already frustrated.

"I'm pretty sure that's it, Hil," I say innocently. "That's got to be the stomach. Yup. I'm one hundred percent sure." (One good thing about hating your former best friend is that you know *exactly* how to push her buttons.)

"It's the brain and you know it." She frowns as her crystalline eyes search the room.

"That's right. See if *David* can tell us. *David* will know. *David* is so *smart.*"

She jabs her hand into the air, savagely arching her back for emphasis. If anyone else tried a move like that they'd look spastic, but Hildie executes it perfectly. An Olympic committee would give her all sixes.

David comes over and says, "Yes," as if he's so tired, he can barely utter the word.

"Kristi keeps saying the brain is the stomach and I can't work with her." Hildie pouts her pink lips at him.

I concentrate my beam on her. One of these days I'll figure out how to make her head explode with my psychic waves.

David nods wisely. "Do you need to start your contemplation early today, Kristi?"

"Yes. I need to go contemplate really, really bad," I say to him. He hands me a slip of paper with the assignment. I take the paper and leave the classroom. I don't even look at stupid Hildie because I can hear her thinking as I go: *Why is she such a bitch?*

THE CONTEMPLATION ROOM

Absolutely no one is allowed to speak in the Contemplation Room. Brian once said he almost named it the Temple, but he thought that the word was too suggestive of religion and he didn't want to make any atheists or agnostics feel excluded from the educational experience here at Journeys.

I slide into my favorite seat next to the window. The tree Hildie mentioned in Morning Meeting looks pink and fluffy, like cotton candy.

I hear the click of a door and see Betty Pasternak, the Self-Expressions teacher, come out of the conference room with the new kid.

He looks around the room for a seat and spies me. I feel him thinking, *Interesting,* which is pretty unusual because most people have a negative reaction when they notice me. I would smile at him if smiling didn't make me look snide, so instead I blink at him. He strolls over.

I've never seen such skinny legs in my life. His knees seem to almost poke through his jeans, and his feet are huge. When he gets to my table he puts his hand on the back of the chair opposite me and raises his orange eyebrows.

I nod.

He sits down and leans forward on his elbows. Up close his acne is quite vibrant. Huge red bumps cover his entire face and neck. Where there aren't fresh pimples there are raised red patches. It makes me feel a little sorry for him. I smell hints of cigarette smoke on him, which I think is kind of cool. I like people who don't do what they're supposed to do. "This place is psycho," he whispers.

"Wait until Processing on Friday," I tell him.

"Processing. Is that when they grind us all into sausage and feed us to our parents?" He grins wickedly.

I stare at him, trying to decide whether he's a nice guy with a dark sense of humor or an ax murderer with a taste for chubby girls. I wait so long to speak, I feel him thinking, *What is her problem?* I'm already blowing it.

"My dad's a vegetarian, so . . ." I taper off. I have no idea why I just said that. My dad is not a vegetarian—at least he wasn't the last time I saw him, two years ago—and it has nothing to do with anything.

I hear a shushing noise. Betty Pasternak is holding her fingers to her lips at us. Some of the other students are looking, too. I hear them thinking, *They're perfect for each other.*

It's not a compliment.

Without even asking, Mallory grabs my notebook and rips a piece of paper out of it. He writes with my pen, *What is the deal with this school?* and pushes it at me.

I write, *It's progressive. Like colon cancer.*

He laughs. *How long have you been here?*

Since ninth grade. I'm a sophomore. How did you end up here?

Got kicked out of my last two schools. I don't deal well with education.

You're in the right place. They don't really have that here.

We trade notes like that until the rest of my Explorations of Nature class gets here to write their daily contemplations. David sees me and comes over, stroking his beard, which means that he expects me to show him my Frost pastiche on anatomy. I show him the paper Mallory and I have been trading back and forth because I know he won't bother to read it. He nods and heads for Hildie's table, where she's staring prettily at her notebook, chewing on the eraser of her pencil with her perfect pearl teeth. David leans over Hildie and looks at her work. I'm pretty sure he's smelling her hair.

He's a teacher? Mallory asks.

He seems to think so, I write back.

By the time the lunch gong rings, I feel as though Mallory and I are almost friends. I even catch him thinking, *She's cool.* It's been ages since anyone thought that about me. Not even Jacob thinks I'm cool. He hangs out with me only because he's so uncool that he doesn't even consider coolness a factor when choosing friends. This is mostly why I tolerate him.

I lead Mallory to the World Bistro (a.k.a. the school cafeteria), where we get in line for the ratatouille. All the meals are cooked by the students in the Culinary Arts class, a requirement I'm putting off until senior year. The last thing my found wardrobe needs is exposure to an open flame. Every week they serve a different nationality of food. Last week we explored the Indian subcontinent; this week we're doing regional French. Next week is supposed to be Scandinavia, but no one is excited about the wonders of pickled fish.

"Uh. Hi, Kristi," I hear lisped behind me.

"Hi, Jacob," I say as I wipe spit droplets off my shoulder. "This is Mallory."

Mallory sticks out his hand toward Jacob, who doesn't even notice the gesture because he's staring at Mallory's acne with unconcealed awe. "How do you do?" Mallory says grimly.

"Hi," Jacob finally says, then looks at me, horror stricken.

I ignore him.

One of the student servers, a freshman with huge cheekbones and a tiny mouth, plunks a bowl of ratatouille onto my tray. "Nice attitude," I tell her.

"Get bit," she sneers.

"Hey, you have a nasty animal clinging to your head," Mallory tells her. "Oh, wait. That's your face."

She doesn't miss a beat. "There's this substance called soap?" She smiles meanly at his acne. "It's widely available in drugstores?"

Mallory narrows his eyes at her.

Her eyes get even narrower.

I like freshmen with spirit.

"Is there someplace where I can smoke?" Mallory asks me. He points at the slop on my tray. "I've lost my appetite."

"Smoking isn't allowed on school property," Jacob says

over his shoulder. He heads for our table, expecting me to follow him. When he sees I'm still standing with Mallory, he stamps his foot.

Mallory rolls his eyes at me.

"Go behind the bushes by the parking lot," I tell him.

He walks away, his tiny butt barely moving. Everyone stares at him as he goes.

"He should really go to a dermatologist," Jacob says as we sit down.

"So?" I ask.

"Maybe his skin would get better if he quit smoking," Jacob says. "Plus, he doesn't look good in white. It creates too much contrast with his acne. And isn't Mallory a girl's name? Did you notice Eva Kearns-Tate looks kind of sick these days? She's ghastly pale and —"

I put on my Maria Callas headphones and tune Jacob out.

OIL SPILL

The best kind of practical joke is one that seems like an act of God. That is the first rule of shenanigans. The second rule is that you have to be present to watch the shit go down. What is the point of engineering a brilliant prank if you're not there to enjoy it? The third rule is that you have to make yourself known to your victim but present yourself as a helpful agent of good, which only heightens the pathos of the whole situation. Finally: never give the same name twice.

My favorite setting for practical jokes is this spot in the park right behind Journeys. The park is bordered by a super-busy concrete bike path. Right where the bike path makes a sharp turn is a spot that has been polished very smooth by lots of feet and tires. It is so smooth, it feels and looks like polished pewter. Just where the concrete is smoothest, there happens to be a very shallow puddle, and in the middle of that puddle, there happens to be an invisible layer of motor oil.

How do I know this?

Because I put it there.

I get a Dixie cup full of water, and I bring my pint of motor oil wrapped in a paper bag. First I pour the water around until it's a thin layer, and then I very carefully dribble oil over the water. Something about the way the water floats over the polished smooth concrete and the way the oil hovers on the water makes this spot the slipperiest surface known to man.

After my setup is complete, I sit under my favorite tree and watch for my next victim. It doesn't always work. Sometimes they're wearing shoes with good treads. Sometimes they miss the puddle. But sometimes everything lines up perfectly.

Today I get a very fat businessman who's walking toward Journeys superduper fast, his tummy jiggling with every step, a folder tucked into his chubby hand. I can see the perspiration marks under his arms as he jogs down the bike path in his fancy dress shoes with the smooth leather soles. He glances at his watch and speeds up. He must be very late for a meeting.

The last thing he needs right now is to fall down.

He doesn't even see it coming. As he rounds the bend, his foot slides out from under him, and he's splayed flat before he can say, "Aaaahh!" His folder goes flying, and suddenly all these papers are whirling around him in a white tornado. "Oh, Jesus!" he cries as he scrambles to his feet. He starts pawing at the air, but most of his papers are halfway to the street. He'll never catch them all.

After a minute or two quietly laughing, I get up to help him pick up the papers. I can move about ten times as fast as he can, and I run over to where the papers are lying in the street gutter. "Oh, thank you, young lady!" he cries. His face is fire red from the exertion, but he manages a smile as I hand him what I've gathered.

"They're probably all out of order, mister," I say. I add the "mister" just so I seem especially young and innocent.

"No matter, dear." He takes them from me, and then we both chase after the stragglers. I find a bunch of them tangled in the lilac bushes near the street corner. Once we get them all together, he smiles at me again. "You're a real peach."

"I like to help people." I beam at him like a cherub who has just dosed on ecstasy.

"What's your name?" he asks as he wipes his forehead with his sleeve.

"Daisy. Daisy Fawn."

He offers me his hand, and we shake. "Thank you, Daisy Fawn."

He walks away, bouncing and jiggling, feeling really positive about the goodness in people. He thinks, *What a dear heart she is. Such a sweetie!*

The irony is delicious.

HOME AT NIGHT

The house is quiet when I get home, but of course there's a note on the fridge. There's always a note.

Dear Kristi,

You could say good morning to your mother, you know.

Use the twenty under the phone and get takeout, but please no pizza. Get something healthy from Zen Palace, OK? I should be home by eleven tonight—at least that's when my shift ends. I have big news to tell you, so please stay up until I get home.

I know we haven't been able to spend much time together, and I want you to know how much I regret that. Soon things are going to get a lot easier for both of us.

Thanks for hanging in there, honey.

And please, order something healthy for dinner. I mean it this time.

I love you,

Mom

Mom might be a little overweight, but she's still an absolute health nut. For my fifth birthday party she got me an all-natural carrot cake from an organic bakery that sweetens everything with honey. Hildie took one bite of it and announced to the room, "Ew! This tastes like bird poop!" She actually knew what bird poop tastes like because she used to let her pet parakeet walk all over her face. She liked how it felt all tickly. Well, it takes only one time for a kid to learn why you don't let your parakeet walk on your face. Everyone at my party knew that story, too, so they knew that she wasn't just making up a colorful metaphor. So for the rest of the day they yelled at me, "Kristi eats bird poop!" You would think my mother would take all this under advisement when selecting the cake for my next birthday, but she did not. She got me a carob-raisin mocha chip, which was as yummy as it sounds.

Thank God at least Mom is even more addicted to coffee than I am. She buys only organic fair-trade beans, so she can rationalize it.

I've been bypassing my mother's health-nut notions for many, many years. My method is nearly perfect. First I call Zen Palace and order steamed broccoli and seared bean curd over brown rice, then I call up Pizza Pal and get the meatiest, treatiest pizza with extra cheese and a large Coke. When the food comes I let Minnie Mouse out of my room. She sits on the couch next to me and eats out of the Zen Palace container while I eat every last piece of cheesy, carby, tangy, saucy pizza. Then we settle in for a night of empty, meaningless, mind-numbing TV.

Usually I start with CNN to see if there are any trapped miners or babies in a well or puppies that have been abused by some crazed farmer in Arkansas. Then I go to the network news magazines to find out what minuscule advancement in cancer research is making headlines this week. Then I go to Fox News to find out how quickly and confidently good-looking retards can lie. And finally I end up on Comedy Central, where I get the news.

Tonight, though, my usual lineup doesn't feel quite distracting enough. I keep thinking about the new kid, Mallory. I like his attitude. He gets kicked out of schools but he doesn't seem to care about that. I think it's kind of cool that he smokes. Maybe I should try it. It would certainly suit my subversive persona. Plus it would kill Mom. She tells me at least once a week about some patient of hers who smokes, and how *if only he wasn't a smoker,* he might have made it out of post-op without getting pneumonia. Mom hates smoking.

Maybe tomorrow Mallory will bum me a cigarette.

Minnie sits on my lap purring contentedly, and I feel warm and snuggly with her. I run my fingers through her feathery neck hair, which puffs out the more I touch it. Minnie is the most beautiful cat I've ever seen. She has long white hair like a Persian, and her face is as slender as the face of a lioness. Her nose is black, which looks really pretty with her white fur, and her topaz yellow eyes sparkle.

I could fall asleep on the couch right here, but I don't want to be in the living room when Mom gets home. She's got a heart-to-heart in mind, and if I can avoid her long enough I might be able to squirm my way out of it. Besides, it would be fatal if she found me on the couch with Minnie.

I scoot Minnie into my room and close the door, then go back to the living room to fold up my pizza box until it's quite tiny. There's not enough garbage to hide it in the kitchen trash, so I have to take it out to the garage.

It's cold in the garage, enough that I can see my breath, even in the dark. It always smells like motor oil and cement in here, and I wrinkle my nose because the smell reminds me of Dad and I don't like being reminded. I try not to look at his workbench, but I can't help it.

The jewelry box he started making for me is still sitting on the shelf above his toolbox. He started it four years ago. I used to love watching him work. He'd get a single bead of sweat between his eyebrows when he cut the pieces with his table saw, and he had a way of sticking his tongue in the corner of his mouth when he was fitting together two pieces of wood. The box was supposed to be my birthday gift when I turned eleven, but he stopped working on it when the lid warped. It doesn't close completely. He said he needed to take the hinges off and plane it down, but Dad's planer needed sharpening, and there was only one place that could do it right, and they were never open when Dad had time off, so my jewelry box just ended up sitting there waiting to be finished. After a few months Dad seemed to forget all about it, but I never did.

I jump when the garage door whirs to life. A thin line of light appears at the bottom, and I can hear the hum of our ancient Volvo. Mom's home. I leap inside, sprint to my room, and lock the door. As I swan dive under the covers, I barely miss Minnie, who has curled up in the folds of my comforter. I bury my face in my pillow and hold my breath so I can listen.

The door to the garage opens and closes. Her keys clang in the bowl she keeps on the table in the hallway. I hear her sigh, and she calls, "Kristi! Come on, let's talk!"

I pretend to be asleep.

I hear a pleased "Oh!" and I realize that she has found the leftover Zen Palace on the coffee table and has probably begun to eat it. Little does she know that it has been thoroughly licked and chewed by a housecat. Gross. I should stop her, but what would I say? "Don't eat that"? "Because I said so"? After a while I hear her heavy footsteps coming down the hallway to my room.

She raps on my door, and Minnie tenses against my leg. I expected Mom to knock, but it still startles me. "Come on! Let's go!" Her mental vibes feel less defeated than usual. In fact, there's a weird quality to her thoughts that I can't identify, and it makes me curious.

"I'm trying to sleep!" I yell at her. "Tell me through the door!"

"I saw you running out of the garage. Get out here." I hear her thinking, *Why is it always a fight?*

"Jesus, Mom. If you had regular hours like other parents . . ." Guilt usually works with her. She's half Jewish, half Greek Orthodox. It's a lethal mix.

Her thoughts twinge with a brief *It's not my fault I have to work so hard*, but she says firmly, "That's what I want to talk about—move it," before stomping down the hallway and into the living room.

I hate talking to my mother. I hate it more than I hate any other part of the day. We always end up fighting because she has no sense of humor at all and she never listens to me.

I tromp down the hallway as loudly as possible. Mom's parked on the couch, one thick leg resting on the glass coffee table as she roots through the Zen Palace container for the pieces of tofu Minnie so lovingly licked and gnawed moments ago. She takes big bites so that her lips have to poof out, which makes her look kind of funny. She's already taken her hair out of the bun she always wears. There's a line from her surgical cap still on her forehead and another line across her nose from her mask. She must have just come from surgery, but her scrubs are clean, so I guess she changed at the hospital, which probably means there was a lot of blood. When I sit on the chair opposite her she raises one arched eyebrow at me. Dad always said she had the eyes of Bette Davis and the lips of Sophia Loren. That was a long time ago, before she started making him feel so small. "Nice of you to put in an appearance," she says through a mouthful of brown rice.

I fold my arms over my chest. "Well? What?"

"No 'How was your day, Mom?' No 'Gee, thanks for bringing me into the world'? All I get is a 'Well? What?'"

"How was your day?"

"Miserable and bloody. How was yours?"

"Splendid. I learned oh so much at 'school.'" I make the quotation marks with my fingers.

She's quiet. This is an old argument. She makes me go to bogus Journeys because she thinks that will help me get into a decent college.

"Kristi, I got some great news yesterday, and I wanted to tell you this morning, but you ran out before I could." She registers the look of relative indifference on my face and adds: "It's great for both of us." She smiles into the Zen Palace carton as she extracts a broccoli floret and pops it into her mouth. She chews, all satisfied as she thinks, *Finally she won't have a reason to be so nasty.* With a full mouth she says, "I got promoted. I'm chief of surgery now." She beams, expecting me to make the connection to how this is great news for me.

"And?"

"Congratulations, Mom," she drones at me.

"Congratulations, Mom," I drone, but then I feel guilty about droning, so I lean over to give her an awkward pat on the shoulder. "Good job."

"This means we'll have more money and I'll have my pick of surgeries. I can arrange my schedule the way I like, so I'll be home for you more."

"For me?"

She nods, smiling with teeth that are almost too big, totally ignoring the crestfallen look on my face.

In a flash I see what this means. No more evenings on the couch with Minnie. No more pizzas. No more news-program nights. I'm going to have to spend time concealing my contempt, which takes a lot of energy because I have a lot of contempt. I sit in silence, absorbing this devastating turn of events, while Mom nibbles on a piece of tofu that has clearly, clearly been chewed thoroughly by my cat and then spit out. I'm so disturbed by what she has told me that I almost miss Mom's first Minnie-related, lung-racking sneeze.

"Ack!" she cries. "I was fine all day!" She pulls her antihistamines out of her pocket and pops one, washing it down with a swill of all-natural root beer.

I feel bad that I let her eat Minnie's leftovers until I hear her thinking, *Chief of surgery! I finally made it.*

She's acting like this promotion is about spending more time with me, but I know the truth. It's all about her ambition.

Why does she have to pretend like that?

CHARACTER EDUCATION

The next Monday at school I can tell Brian has something very special for us at Morning Meeting, because he is standing in the middle of the circle of students beaming at us in a particularly maniacal way. He has on a tunic from India with a line of elephants along the bottom and loose-fitting linen pants with Birkenstocks. His thin, longish hair is pulled into a tiny ponytail at the back of his head, and his face is shiny with grease. He's holding some papers tightly in his hand and slowly turning around and around, waiting for us to focus. I'm standing with my arms folded as Luciano Pavarotti and Mirella Freni blare the death scene of *La bohème* in my ears. I feel a tap on my shoulder. I expect Jacob Flax but smile when I see Mallory standing behind me. He has on all white again except for the green pot leaf on his T-shirt. White must be a thing with him.

"Hey," I say. I take off one of my earphones so that I can hear Pavarotti and Mallory at the same time.

"Cool outfit."

He's referring to the skirt I made out of a torn awning from a dumpster behind a lawn and garden store and the shredded office shirt that I made from one of the many pieces of clothing my wayward father left behind. "Thanks."

"Where do you shop?"

"Trash cans, mostly," I say.

I can hear him thinking, *Cool.*

Brian starts clapping at all of us, pretending to applaud when really he's just trying to get our attention. Gusty Peterson starts clapping, too, and because everyone wants to be just like him, all the other students start clapping. Pretty soon the entire activity center is filled with an ear-crashing ovation. Sam Juarez starts catcalling and pumping his fist in the air, and then Jacob Flax jumps up and down for joy. I shoot a glance at Mallory, who is staring at the show with his mouth open. His eyes slide over to me. "Did everyone drop acid before I got here?"

"We're just excited because the mother ship is landing today."

"Oh good, I love a mass suicide." He grins that wicked grin that makes me a little nervous and a little happy because finally there's someone in my school as dark and twisted as I am.

Finally the room settles down and Brian smiles warmly. "Welcome to Journeys! How is everyone?" he asks, and then for some crazy reason he pauses as if expecting an answer.

Mallory shouts, "I'm a little hung-over."

Everyone laughs.

Brian raises one eyebrow, but his insane smile is undiminished. "I have a special treat for everyone. Jacob Flax's self-improvement project inspired me." Jacob, who is standing by the vending machines, swells with pride. "So I thought I'd institute a new character education unit."

Everyone groans. Jacob's face falls and he looks around the room nervously.

Brian holds up the papers in his hand. "The faculty worked hard last night on this project, and I really think that once you understand what it's about, you're really going to love it." He strolls over to the bulletin boards on the wall and tacks up the papers. "Each of you has been assigned a peer partner, and together you're going to work on building your characters."

Mallory utters a tiny groan that reminds me of Minnie Mouse complaining when her litter box is full of turds. It captures my sentiment perfectly.

"You will be given a series of questionnaires and projects to complete together throughout the term. The faculty has made suggestions, posted here, for who you should work with this year. If you want to change partners, clear your choice with someone on the faculty committee. There are a few rules, however. You must work with someone you don't know well. You cannot work with someone in your own grade. You must work with someone who's in the same free period as you. And finally, you should work with someone of a different gender."

I look around the room. All the students look as if Brian

has just announced that we're being shipped off to concentration camps.

I put both my headphones on and turn up the volume of *la bohème*'s final moments on earth. Mirella Freni hacks up a lung while Pavarotti wails out a gorgeously deafening lament. It's great music for watching everyone mill around like automatons, getting their assignments and finding their partners. Opera is the perfect soundtrack for the tragedy of modern life.

I manage not to talk to anyone until lunch, but of course, Jacob is the one to break my winning streak.

"Are you excited about the character education project, Kristi?" Jacob asks me in the lunch line. A tiny glob of his spit careens through the air, barely missing the Norwegian smoked salmon and cold potato wraps on my plate. His eyes fall onto my breasts and I catch a mental glimpse of me taking a bubble bath in the middle of a poppy field. "I'm working with Ebony Roosevelt," he says. "I hope she doesn't want to change partners."

"Just try not to spit on her."

"Right," he says. "Are you psyched about your partner?"

"I'm not working with anyone," I say, because I don't intend to. They can flunk me if they want to, but I consider my character ready-made.

He cocks his head sympathetically. "So Gusty Peterson didn't want to work with you, huh?"

I freeze. I had no idea I'd been assigned to Gusty. He makes me a little nervous, sure, but all beautiful people make me nervous. Their unfair power over the rest of us mere mortals is daunting, but that doesn't mean I *want* them or *lust* after them or anything. It just means that I don't trust them to use their beauty for good rather than evil. And like most beautiful people, Gusty Peterson is a mentally stunted egotistical poser.

And he's my character education partner? Jesus. What will I wear?

I'm staring in shock at Jacob until I hear, "Keep the line moving!" The spunky little freshman snarls as she doles out another cold potato wrap. Her hair is crammed into short pigtails, and she has a huge zit on her perky little nose. "I don't have all day," she says to me.

"Norwegian cuisine is awesome!" I say, and give her a super-enthusiastic thumbs-up. "Are you serving endangered whale next? Yum!"

"Wouldn't eating whale make you a cannibal?" She sneers at my big hips.

"You should really harpoon that zit on your nose," I tell her before moving on.

"Good one, Kristi," Jacob says, tripping after me. "So I joined Pumps and Rips yesterday. You should see some of the guys in there! I mean, they're like Arnold Schwarzenegger or something. I felt a little feeble when I got there last night, but then one of the guys was super nice to me and showed me how to work the nautilus machine. And did you notice my hair?" He runs his fingers clumsily through his bangs as we sit down.

"What about it?"

"I washed it, and I even used conditioner!" he says, all excited. "You're right— it really looks good now, but I think I'm going to get some gel to keep it out of my eyes."

"Uh-huh."

"What do you think about highlights? Is it okay for a guy to get highlights?"

"Jesus, Jacob."

"Hey." Mallory plunks down next to Jacob, who leans away from him.

"Hey," I say, lifting up the potato wrap and letting it fall to my tray with a wet, disgusting *thunk*.

"The food here is multifariously nefarious," Mallory says in a gravy-like voice that should be on the radio.

"I like trying new things," Jacob mutters before taking a tiny bite of smoked salmon.

"I'd kill for a Tater Tot," I say.

Jacob widens his white-blue eyes. "Do you know how *fattening* those are?"

"Want to go have a smoke?" Mallory asks, raising his eyebrows at me.

"She doesn't smoke," Jacob says, nodding secretly at me so I'll back him up. His mind whispers, *Stay with me, stay with me.*

"Sure," I say to Mallory, and get up from the table. I figure it's about time my rebellion took on more conventional overtones. I follow Mallory toward the door, kind of laughing at the weird leaning way he walks, as though he were moving through very deep water. We're almost out the Bistro door when I feel a hand on my arm. I turn and there's Gusty Peterson, all six feet of him, with his electric eyes and tan skin and golden hair and perfect straight teeth. "Hey," he says, and licks his firm lips. I can feel him thinking, *Totally sick.*

"Hi," I say, but I don't smile. Mallory stands just to the side, shifting from one foot to the other, waiting for me.

"So I guess we're working together, huh?" Gusty says. His eyes trail slowly down my shredded shirt as he thinks, *God, her outfit is . . .* , but he seems to catch himself. "Do you want to meet up during free period tomorrow and we can go over our first assignment?"

"Where?"

"How about in here?" He raises his eyebrows, and somehow that makes me notice his perfectly chiseled cheekbones. He turns to look warily at Mallory.

He's beautiful, that's for sure. Dangerous as hell and kind of dumb, but beautiful.

"Okay, I'll see you in here tomorrow," I tell him, careful to keep my voice nice and smooth.

He nods at Mallory without even cracking a grin and goes back to the beautiful-people table to sit with Hildie and Eva Kearns-Tate, who turns to give me a narrow-eyed stare.

"Who's that guy?" Mallory asks as we stride out of the Bistro.

"Gusty Peterson."

"Gusty? As in breezy?"

"As in Gustav. His dad's from Sweden."

"Oh." We walk down the empty hallway in silence. "And that chick Hildie is his sister, huh?"

"Yeah," I say sadly, because I'm remembering. Back when Hildie was fun, we used to walk through the streets of our town pretending she was blind. She could even cross one eye slightly. I'd lead her around, saying, "Step! Step! Okay, red light." And she'd follow me, her hands stuck out in front of her. Sometimes grownups would come up to us and ask if we needed help. A few times Hildie would intentionally bump into them and then pretend she really got hurt, and they'd be horrified and say, "I'm so sorry, honey—are you okay? Oh my God!" And I'd yell at them, "Just go, okay? We're fine!" They'd hurry away feeling like monsters, and Hildie and I would laugh like drunk hyenas.

"What's Hildie short for?" Mallory asks as he guides me out the door with his hand on my waist. I don't like the way he looks, but I like the way he touches me.

"What? Oh, Hildegard." I blink because the bright sun hurts my eyes.

"Holy hell! I thought my name was bad!"

"It is. Aren't you named after the sister on *Family Ties*?"

"I see you like prehistoric sitcoms. That's funny." He kicks at a pile of tiny gravel in the parking lot and it scatters. "I'm named after the poet. You know. *Le Morte d'Arthur*?"

"Oh. You think your name has dignity. I get it."

"And I guess you're working with that Gusty guy on the character education assignment?" Mallory asks me, his voice weirdly careful. I can feel uneasiness in his mind, but I don't understand it.

I don't answer. I don't want to talk about the Petersons anymore.

We sit on the grass behind the thick bushes that line the parking lot. Soon winter will be here and all the leaves will be gone, so we'll have to find another place to smoke.

Mallory shakes two cigarettes out of his pack with a flick of his wrist, lights his first and then mine. I take tiny little puffs, almost as if I'm kissing the filter.

Instantly my lungs shrink to the size of blisters.

"You don't have to smoke the whole thing," Mallory tells me when he sees my face, which is probably purple.

"Okay," I say, and grind it out on a rock. So much for my refurbished rebellion. I'll do something less horrible, like facial scarification.

"So, Kristi Carmichael. What's your story?" He sucks so hard on the cigarette, his cheeks pull inward.

"Which part do you want?"

"The middle."

"Puberty, then. I went from a training bra to a C cup in eleven months."

"Jesus, was anyone injured?"

"I blinded a man."

"Lucky bastard." He smiles shyly at the ground.

I get a flash of him imagining what my ginormous gazungas would feel like against his acne-scarred face, and suddenly I wish I hadn't mentioned them. It makes me nervous, sitting here with Mallory, but not the kind of nervous Gusty makes me. It's the kind of nervous that makes me afraid that the first person I actually want to be friends with in this miserable school has something else in mind.

I scoot away from him a tiny distance and cross one ankle over the other. "Let's see. That was eighth grade, when I was still going to public school. Hildie and I were still friends."

Our conversation drops a beat while Mallory decodes my body language. I moved away from him only two inches, but that's enough. He gets the picture. "You were *friends* with her?" he asks nonchalantly, then pulls in a ton of smoke and blows it out violently. "She doesn't seem like the kind of person you'd hang out with."

"Why not?"

"I don't know." He waves his cigarette over my outfit. "You're so creative and nonconformist. She's so . . ."

"Popular?"

"Yeah, I guess."

"Well, a lot can happen in a few years."

"That's for damn sure," he says. His mind is suddenly filled with angry vibes. He tamps out his cigarette and leans back on his elbows, staring at his big feet.

"What's your story?" I ask him. "Tell me the middle."

"The middle," he says thoughtfully. "The *mmmm*iddle," he says again, as if he's tasting the word for the very first time and he isn't sure he likes it. He glances at me sideways, and there's so much naked pain in his mind that I have to turn away. Reaching into the rear pocket of his white jeans, he pulls out his wallet. From it he takes a small creased picture of a little redheaded boy with a big smile and creamy smooth skin.

It's Mallory. I don't say anything. I feel jumpy because I want to make him feel better but there isn't any way. He used to be cute; now he's hideous, and he knows it.

I look at the photo again—the sunny smile, the freckles, the scampish glint in his eyes. There's something very familiar about this picture, and I slap my forehead when it hits me. "Oh my God! You were the Wheat Puffs kid!"

"I was the *Honey Nut* Wheat Puffs kid," he corrects me.

"You were a child model?"

"Yeah, for about two years, before—" He doesn't have to continue. I know what happened. Puberty.

How many lives must Puberty destroy before it is finally stopped?

"People used to stop my mom and me in the street to say how adorable I was. Within two years I became the kid people try *not* to stare at. I'm like the Elephant Man."

"Have you tried going to a dermatologist?"

"I've tried everything except for this really nasty pill that has God-awful side effects. My mom doesn't want me to do it."

"What are the side effects?"

"It can make your hair fall out. It can hurt your vision, increase your cholesterol, damage your liver, cause depression and, some say, suicide . . ." With one hand he pulls his pony-tail holder out of his hair and shakes his thick long hair loose. "My mom has a fear of medications."

I want to ask him if his mom has disfiguring acne, because if she doesn't, she should keep her phobias to herself. But it's not my business. I shift my position, and I catch his thoughts noting the way my breasts move. I should start wearing those super-supportive bras that would make a supermodel feel frumpy. At least then I could be friends with guys without them mentally picturing my breasts bobbing in ocean waves, like Mallory is doing right now.

Christ, my gazungas are such a curse.

If we're going to hang out together, I know I should make things clear, but I don't really know how. It always seemed like Hildie could tell a guy her feelings with a simple turn of her head. This is the first time I've ever had to make my feelings known to a guy, and the only way I know how to do it is to be direct. "Anyway, I'm glad you came here. I needed a friend."

He's quiet for a while, his smile wan as he digests the information I've given him. Finally he takes a quick, deep breath and holds his fist out to me. I touch my knuckles to his and we smile. "Ditto. Friends." *For now,* I hear him think.

We hear the bell ring for next period, and we stroll into the building, both of us quietly thinking.

Him: *Maybe she'll change her mind.*

Me: *Poor Mallory.*

GUSTY

I'm standing outside the Bistro, hugging my notepad and looking at Gusty through the glass door. He's slumped at the table tapping his fingertips on the edge of his book. He has on a baseball hat today, but the brim is cocked to the side so that I can see only the bottom half of his face. His shoulders are very square, but there's a curve of muscle in his arm. He's wearing unlaced high-tops and jeans that make him look very relaxed and very sexy.

Not that I want him or anything.

Not that I spent an extra hour today choosing the perfect outfit — my super-tight denim skirt that I hand-painted with stars and galaxies and a sequined tank top that hugs my ginormous boobs in just the right way. It wasn't because of him that I gave myself a headache from standing too close to the mirror applying eyeliner and mascara. And the fact that I went to the drugstore last night to find the absolute perfect shade of raisin red lip-gloss is completely coincidental.

I was out. I needed more.

Even if I did put a little extra effort into my appearance, it doesn't matter, because I have the sad privilege of hearing his thoughts about me and he always thinks the same thing: that I'm sick.

So why do I try?

Because deep down in the dark corners of my mind I have to admit that I still have the eensiest-weensiest bit of a crush on him, even if he is a poser moron who is too wrapped up in his looks.

I remember the day my mild interest in Gusty morphed into an evil crush with devil horns and a forked tail. I was over at Hildie's house. She and I were lying on the floor reading her mom's *Glamour* about how to give a guy good oral sex, which we thought was another term for phone sex. So you can imagine our confusion. I heard Gusty's feet on the stairs and whispered to Hildie, "Ugh. Your brother's here." We just had time to flip the magazine over to the horoscopes before Gusty made it to the doorway. He had on a sweaty T-shirt, and he was breathing hard from skateboarding home. He was holding a soda, and I noticed that his hand was big enough to cover almost the whole can. Then I noticed how tan his arms were, and then my eyes traveled up to his, and with a shock I saw that he was looking right at me. His eyes were so intense that the rest of his face, the rest of the room, faded to the background so that all I saw were those green pinpoints. The look he gave me did something to me deep inside, and suddenly I was shivering a little. I still shiver every time I remember it.

"Hey," he said to me. There was something private in the way he said it, as though he was trying to talk in such a way that only I could hear. I knew that one word contained a memory we shared: *the two of us, behind the shed in his backyard.*

"Hey," I said.

"Get out of here, *Lusty,*" Hildie spat. "We're busy."

He walked away without once looking at her. His eyes were on me for the longest possible time, until he disappeared behind his bedroom door.

For weeks after, I'd replay that one little word over and over in my mind. I imagined him whispering it just before he kissed me. *Hey.* I imagined him shouting it at me through a rainstorm. I heard him say it just as I was dropping off to sleep, and it would wake me up. *Hey, Kristi. Hey.*

That one word tormented me so much that one day I put on my favorite jeans with the unicorns embroidered on the back pockets and my pink tank top with the beading along the neckline, slid on a dozen silver bracelets from Mom's jewelry drawer, and went over to the Petersons' when I knew Hildie was at gymnastics. Ignoring the voice in my mind telling me, *There's no way a guy that hot would ever like you,* I knocked on the door. I concentrated on keeping my feet attached to the front step as I listened to him barrel down the stairs. "Who is it?" he called through the door.

"K-Kristi," I said, and I didn't even care that I'd stammered.

He opened the door and there he was, looking at me, and I looked at him.

"Hey," he said, and swallowed really hard.

"Hi," I said.

When did he get so tall? I wondered as I took him in: the scab on his arm he'd gotten skateboarding, the twitch in his lip, the curly gold hair that hung in his eyes, the white downy fuzz along his jaw line that was trying, in the most exquisite way, to become a beard.

We didn't smile. We didn't speak. We just stood there. Looking.

I tilted my head. I didn't know what I was telling him by tilting my head, but I knew he'd understand.

He took a step toward me.

I took a step forward.

We were close enough to feel the heat of each other's bodies.

And I knew, I was certain, dead sure, that he was going to kiss me. I closed my eyes and I waited for it. I closed my eyes the same way I'd done that day behind the garden shed. I waited and waited, until I opened my eyes again and saw that he'd turned pale.

"Uh," he said, "Hildie's not home." He gripped the door-knob behind him and squeezed it so hard that his whole hand turned white.

"Oh" was all I could say. And that's when I got my very first real psychic vibe, though it took me a long time to believe it. I distinctly heard him think, *She's even sicker up close.*

And I watched as he shrank back into the house and closed the door between us.

That closed door hurt me like a brick in the face. I'd made a complete fool of myself. I was so stupid to believe he could ever like me.

I couldn't go to the Petersons' house after that, and soon Hildie was finding excuses not to come to my house. The only place I ever saw Gusty was at school, and he seemed to agree with me that it was best if we pretended we didn't see each other at all.

And today I'm supposed to meet with Gusty for character education. Finally, proof that there is a God and he is a total sadist.

I'm standing outside the Bistro door staring at Gusty like a stalker perv, but I can't make my feet move toward him. He's too much. The loose way he sits, his long, muscular legs, his baggy jeans, the shine of the sunlight on the pale hair along his arms, his tan skin, that amazing curve in his jaw line, the way he bites his lower lip, his voice, his smell. Too much. Way too much.

And I can't stand to hear the way he thinks about me. It hurts too much.

I have a simple solution.

I put on my headphones, turn Placido Domingo way, way up.

And then I run away.

Cowardice is underrated.

Or maybe it isn't, because while I'm standing in the lunch line waiting for my serving of congealed pickled herring, I feel a tap on my shoulder. I turn around and there's Gusty, his bottom lip sticking out and his eyebrows jammed together. I'm too nervous to get a clear read on his thoughts, but I can tell he's pissed.

"Hi," I say. I can usually put on a pretty convincing fake confidence, but at the moment I'm about as solid as the fish jelly that has been slapped onto my tray.

"We were supposed to meet during free period this morning, right?" he asks, but it's not really a question.

"Em—"

"Were you out smoking cigarettes with that redheaded guy?" The green of his eyes burns at me.

"I forgot, I'm sorry."

"If you'd rather work with him than me—"

"No!" I almost shout before I remember to act nonchalant.

"Jesus, you freak, will you move your ass?" yells the nasty little freshman. She's holding a slimy spoon covered with fish flakes. "I have fish to dispense."

"Your sex life is not my concern," I tell her before walking to my table. Gusty follows closely behind all the way. I can feel him there. I sense him. The only psychic vibe I get from him is anger—wordless, annoyed anger that I wasted his time.

I sit down across from Jacob Flax, who, amazed by Gusty's presence at our lowly table, launches into an intense friend-making mission. "Hi, Gusty! How's it going?"

"Okay," Gusty says, still glaring at me. He sits next to me and just stares, waiting for me to speak.

Jacob, clueless as ever, starts spitting. "I notice your hair is very blond. Say, do you think it's okay for a guy to get highlights? I was thinking about getting highlights myself but I was wondering — maybe it's not very masculine. But perhaps you've gotten highlights. I don't mean to insult you."

"I spend a lot of time in the sun," Gusty tells him before leaning against me so that I have no way of avoiding him. "Listen, if you don't want to work with me, just say so, okay?"

I am temporarily rendered mute by the awesome feeling of his hard body pushing against my soft body. I can't even chew my fish, and that's not just because it's disgusting, though disgust is certainly a factor. I swallow hard, take a big gulp of milk to wash the fish down all the way so that my breath won't smell bad, and then whisper, "How about we meet after school?"

Now I can manage to glance at him. He's looking at me with his head tilted to one side and he's biting his lip. I try to read his thoughts, but it's hard to do with him so close to me that I can smell him — a sharp mix of peppermint and polished leather.

Gusty has always smelled like that.

He looks at me distrustfully but nods. "Okay, I'll meet you *right here* after school."

"Okay," I croak just as Mallory walks up holding a tray full of weird potato salad.

"Hey," he says, but his voice sounds deflated. His eyes, which are the only part of his face not covered with acne, look at Gusty with dread.

Gusty stands and eyes Mallory right back. There's some kind of primate-level contest going on, and it's one that Jacob dearly wishes he was a part of. Finally Gusty sort of tosses his chin back, like a backwards nod at Mallory, and Mallory backwards nods back. Jacob gives a little wince as Gusty finally walks off. "Okay!" Jacob calls after him. "It was good talking to you, Gusty! I think I'll spend more time in the sun and see how that works!"

Mallory sits down next to me just in time to get sprayed in the face by Jacob saying "works."

"Dude! You have *got* to do something about that!" he says, wiping himself off before giving my arm a little squeeze. "Heya," he says to me. "What is the deal with that mean little freshman serving the food? She just suggested I improve my looks by submerging my face in acid."

"She's a total bitch. I love her," I say, but I can't tear my eyes from Gusty as he walks away.

"Mark my words," Mallory says. Something in his dark thoughts makes me look at his face. "She will pay."

I'm glad he's thinking about the spunky freshman and not me, because there's a devious plan turning over in his mind.

It's not without my heart in my mouth that I go to the Bistro for the third time today. I'm sweating a whole lot, and the only thing that keeps my jaw from trembling is biting my lip a little too hard. When I walk through the door Gusty watches me from under his baseball hat so I can't tell what his expression is. As I sit down across from him, I listen hard for his thoughts, and all I can get is *Why is everything so difficult with her?*

When you're psychic and your character education partner

is mad at you, the best policy is to get down to business. "What's our assignment?"

He hands me a piece of paper with a single sentence written at the top: *For each partner, working together, please make a list of your ten greatest personal attributes.*

"This school blows," I say.

"I kind of like it," he says cheerfully. I search his mind, but I don't get any word thoughts. Maybe he's trying not to be mad at me anymore. He takes a pencil from his backpack and makes a line down the center of the paper. "Who first?"

"You go."

"Okay." He looks at me, the pencil poised above the paper, and waits, his pale yellow eyebrows raised.

"What?" I say.

"What are my ten best personal attributes?"

"How should I know?"

"You can't think of *one* good thing to say about me?" He blinks at me, a little hurt for some reason.

I can think of about a hundred ways he's the hottest guy I've ever laid eyes on, but I'm pretty sure that's not the assignment. I feel in the back of his mind the word *sick* forming. Before he can think it all the way I blurt out, "You're enthusiastic."

"*Enthusiastic?*" He seems disappointed, but he writes it down. I notice that he spells it with a *z*, so obviously spelling is not his forte. "What else?"

"Can't you think of one?"

He crams the pencil into his mouth and spins it on his

tongue. It reminds me of the way he looked when we were kids and we used to play video games together. "I'm really good with my hands," he finally says. "Did you ever see the birdhouse I made for my dad? I carved birds and pinecones on the side. No birds live in it, but my dad says they would crap all over it anyway."

"Okay, put 'good with hands.'"

It takes him a long time to write it, which reminds me again of how dumb he always was. But I guess that's not his fault, just like it's not my fault I'm not gorgeous.

"I have another one I'm good at," he says eagerly. "I'm a total rasta on my board."

"You're a what on your what?"

"I rule as a skater. I can ride almost any trick switch, except for the darkslide and the flamingo. I can do a sex change totally diamondz, and I've almost perfected my pop shove-it underflip."

"What language are you speaking?"

"Skater." He grins, aware that I've caught him showing off.

Something about the sheepish way he's looking at me makes me laugh. "This will go faster if you stick to English."

"Gnarly, Betty," he says quietly.

We go back and forth, thinking of all his best qualities, until we come up with this list:

1. *Enthuziastic*
2. *Good with hands*
3. *Skating switch stance, both street and vert styles*

4. *Good with dogs*

5. *Good listener*

6. *Generous*

7. *Popular*

8. *Tall*

9. *Friendly*

10. *Observant*

"That's ten. Now you." He pauses, pressing his lips together really hard like he always does when he swallows. It actually makes him look less cute than he really is and gives the impression that he's a little insecure, which I suppose is possible, though I don't know what he has to feel insecure about other than the fact that he's not terribly smart. At least, he's not really book smart, but that doesn't necessarily make him dumb, I guess.

"What's your greatest attribute?" he asks me, and then I swear to God his eyes slip all over my boobs like a bar of soap.

I raise one eyebrow at him. He turns totally red, even redder than my raisin red lip-gloss, and I shift in my chair so that my shirt poofs out a little. I say pointedly, "I'm *smart.*"

"Smart," he says, and writes it down.

"I'm creative," I say, and suddenly I feel a little weepy for no reason. "I don't like this assignment," I tell him.

"What else do you like about yourself?" He presses his pencil eraser into his chin and waits. I remember this about him, too. He's quiet, and he watches people a lot. I try to hear what he's thinking, but he doesn't seem to be thinking anything other than *Let's get this done.*

I shake my head. I don't want to admit to the cutest guy in school that I don't like very much about myself, but if I don't say anything, he'll know anyway. "I'm good at practical jokes," I say lamely.

"What kind of practical jokes?" He straightens up in his chair.

"Stealth ones. I'm a master."

"Maybe sometime you'll show me one," he says.

"When you least expect it," I say with an outlaw smile.

He looks at me, one eye cocked in a kind of grin, and I get all blustery.

I don't want to be blustery. I don't want to be sitting here with Gusty Peterson making me blustery. I just want to go home and be with my cat, alone, where I don't have to worry about what anyone is thinking, where I don't have to spend all this energy being nonchalant.

He writes down "Stealth practical jokes," and says, "What else?"

I'm quiet again, trying hard to keep my face from showing how stirred up I'm getting.

He watches me as he taps his pencil eraser against his perfectly chiseled cheekbone. Finally he says, "How about I come up with a few?"

I shrug.

He holds the paper so that I can't see it and starts writing.

Just then Eva Kearns-Tate, a.k.a. Evil Incarnate, walks into the Bistro with Mallory.

Mallory?

Yes, Mallory.

Next to each other, Mallory and Eva look like two praying mantises on the Atkins Diet.

Eva is obviously anorexic and the whole school knows it. Even from far away I can see the blue veins under her porcelain skin, and her cheekbones jut out so sharply, they look like they're trying to escape from her face. She's gorgeous still, but if she keeps it up she'll start to look really unhealthy.

When Mallory sees me he gives me a covert little wave and I nod at him, wondering what in hell's name he's doing here with the second most beautiful, evilest girl in school. I notice she's carrying a slip of paper, and I realize that, of course, the all-knowing faculty paired the most physically unappealing guy with the most self-centered girl to ever flip her hair. They stroll over to us casually. Evil smiles at Gusty privately. "Hi," she says to him, completely ignoring me.

"Hi, Evie," Gusty says, but his eyes are trained on Mallory like two cruise missiles. I hear him thinking, *Stay away from her.*

"Hi, Eva!" I say to her, and smile really sarcastically.

Her dark eyes settle on me in such a way that if I wasn't well insulated with a layer of fat, I'd probably get hypothermia. "Character education should be just the ticket for you, Kristi. Maybe you'll learn some manners."

"She just said hi," Gusty points out, which amazes me. I never expect to see the ranks of the cool divided.

The fact that Gusty stood up for me just makes her madder. "Nice outfit, Kristi," she says. "Did you make it yourself?"

"Yes I did, thanks for asking. And how's your diet going? Are you down to a size negative one yet?"

She doesn't answer. She doesn't have to. She merely looks at my round, soft belly and smiles.

"Uh . . ." Mallory says, and pulls on Eva's sleeve.

Eva tilts her head to one side and gives Gusty a sexy smile that would make a jet engine stutter. He nods at her, but his eyes are on Mallory, and they're burning with an emotion I've never once seen in Gusty's friendly face. Hatred. He hates Mallory, probably because he thinks he's putting the moves on Evil. Oh, the irony.

Mallory and Eva walk to a table across the room.

Gusty looks at me and I smile knowingly. I could help him out by telling him that Mallory, as far as I know, is inexplicably interested in me instead of the she-demon, but why should I help? He thinks I'm sick.

"One of these days you and Eva need to put away your weapons and call a truce," Gusty says.

"What for?"

"What's the point of fighting all the time?" he says simply, then turns back to the paper and starts to write again. All I can hear in his thoughts is *The sooner we get this done, the sooner we can get out of here.*

It really hurts my feelings that he wants so badly to get away from me, but I try not to show it.

When Gusty is done writing, he bites his lip. He looks at me nervously as he drops the paper onto the table to show me what he's written.

1. Smart
2. Creative
3. Stealth practical jokes
4. Funny
5. Independent
6. Amazing dresser
7. Interesting
8. Good at math
9. Defiant

And that's it. There's no number ten.

My first reaction is to feel flattered. He wrote some pretty nice things about me, and maybe some of them are even true, but then I get a flash of myself through his eyes and I look monstrous. My arms are round and fat, my eyes are freakishly huge, and my boobs are enormous and sloshing around like two sacks of water.

He wrote those nice things about me to get this over with so that he can skateboard home and probably play video games. So I just look at him, trying not to cry, and I say, "That looks okay. For number ten put 'Impervious to false flattery.'"

His eyebrows crash together as he studies me. "Well, I had something in mind for number ten, but . . ."

"That's okay. Just put 'Impervious to false flattery,'" I say, because at all costs I must protect myself from number ten.

"I'm not putting that." He watches me angrily for a second, and I can see the color magenta slowly crawling up his neck to take over his face. I totally have his number and he's embarrassed now. He stabs letters onto the paper, then folds it and gets up from the table to leave.

"What did you write?"

"Why do you want to know, since you're so impervious to flattery?" He crunches the paper in his fist and presses it against his leg, thinking, *Bitch*. That's probably what he wrote. He wrote that I'm a bitch.

"Give me the paper, Gusty!" I yell. From across the room, Eva's mean voice sears my mind: *She's such a drama queen.*

Gusty sees Mallory and Eva staring at us, and this makes him even madder. "I didn't write anything!" he says, so I have no choice but to lunge at him and rip the paper out of his hands. I get only half of it, but I get the half with number ten and I unfold it to see that he wrote, "Beautiful."

He wrote *beautiful?*

By the time I catch my breath and look up from this mind-blowing, confusing, earthshattering, and beautiful word, he has walked out the Bistro door and there's no way I could ever summon the courage to catch up with him.

Anyway, what would I say?

It's a cruel lie. It must be.

BIG NEWS FROM AUNT ANN

I'm just going to put it out of my mind, that's all. I'm not going to think about Gusty Peterson or his mean flattery or the way he stormed out of the Bistro with no explanation. I will not think about the weird way my heart won't stop pounding, and I especially will not think about the piece of torn paper that I folded up and placed in my porcelain box with the painted violets on it that I got from Aunt Ann. The piece of paper is there; it's safe. That's all I need to know about it. So I'm not going to think about it anymore. Because it's a lie.

It's a cruel lie.

I grab an all-natural root beer from the fridge and open the door to my bedroom to let Minnie out, and then I sit on our stuffy leather couch with my feet on the coffee table and settle in for some crappy TV. Minnie pads down the hallway, silently cuddles into the crook of the couch, and purrs like a lawn mower. It's hard to really relax because I have to cram an entire evening of fun with Minnie into the two hours between school ending and Mom coming home.

Her schedule has become annoyingly reliable. I thought with her new job that she would still work late because she's a career-obsessed workaholic, but no sirree. She comes home at 5:30 on the dot and expects us to eat dinner together, which means we park our wide loads on the sofa and watch TV news programs while we eat takeout. I usually feel her thinking, *Why can't we talk?* And I don't really know why we can't, but we never have been able to. Dad was always the one I talked with, sometimes about stuff I did *not* want to know about. To give you an idea, here's a smattering of Dad's greatest hits:

"The passion leaves a marriage surprisingly quickly, Kristi. It can be hard on a man when his wife is more ambitious in her career than he is. It's very emasculating. And God, don't ever humiliate your spouse. She once told our colleagues how long it took me to insert my first vascular shunt when we were interning together. That is a difficult procedure, Kristi, and it has nothing to do with the size of your hands. She was always saying how much better women are at surgery because their hands are smaller, which is just not true. A lot of women have a tremor in their hands — you watch. See if I'm right."

I watched. I saw that he was right.

The worst stuff was what he didn't tell me, but I could catch only little hints of it because it was before I'd fully developed my talent. But I knew. He felt desperate. He felt trapped. Confined. He needed out. My mother had worn him thin.

And when the last lawsuit happened, that was all it took for him to snap.

I guess I don't blame Morgan Stewart's family. He was a college track star who held the record for the long jump. So when he came into the emergency room with chest pain, Dad thought he'd suffered a collapsed lung.

It was all Dad talked about:

"I mean, sometimes the symptoms don't add up, you know? Even brilliant diagnosticians can be fooled. Maybe I should have called an internist to double-check, but everything, and I mean *everything,* pointed to a simple collapsed lung, which can happen in tall, thin young men. Surgery is rarely indicated. Radiology was busy, and we had that hit and run to worry about, so I had him lie down in an observation room to wait until we could get an x-ray, just for a couple minutes." He always stopped here, the lines in his forehead deepening. It was like he was trying to remember it in just the right order to bring the kid back alive. But the story always ended the same way. He would shake his head in disbelief and say, "A complication from undiagnosed Marfan syndrome. Thoracic aortic dissection. Boom. And he died."

He died.

He told me this story over and over again for weeks. At first it seemed like he was trying to explain it to me so that I would understand and forgive him, but I forgave him so many times that I finally realized he was telling the story so that he could forgive himself. But he never could.

If that had been the first lawsuit, it would have been okay, but it was Dad's third. His malpractice insurance got so high that he couldn't pay it. The hospital couldn't keep him on staff without insurance, so they forced him to resign. Dad just accepted it. He didn't even fight it because he believed he deserved it.

I don't know. Maybe he did.

The doorbell screams at me. I jump, and Minnie digs her claws into my lap. I have to breathe for a second before I am calm enough to turn down the TV and answer the door.

Aunt Ann is standing on the doorstep, her face pinched with anxiety. Her face is so narrow that she almost doesn't look normal, but that's not her only problem. She looks like she's been ravaged by a hurricane. Her curly brown hair forms a tangled crown on her head. Her huge ratty coat hangs on her tiny body, and she holds her beaten satchel against her chest as if it is made of Teflon and she is expecting enemy fire.

Don't worry. She's fine. She always looks like this.

"Is your mom home?" she asks with her wavery voice. She is terrified to death of my mother.

"No."

She heaves a huge sigh of relief and barges into the living room. She drapes herself over the back of the couch and leans her elbow on the armrest. Aunt Ann has never used furniture right. "I'm so tired! Don't ever try yoga."

"Uh, there's really no danger of that."

"How's things?"

"Okay," I say, and then I wince because of course I sound fake.

"What's wrong?" She stands up too fast and gets a head

rush but keeps talking. "Are you feeling all right? You don't have another one of those headaches, do you? You should have yourself checked for allergies! I should talk to your mother," she says with trepidation. She hates talking to my mother.

"I'm fine." She squints at me because she can tell I'm lying. "It's no big deal. It's just that I've been partnered for a project at school with Gusty Peterson."

"Why do I know that name?"

"Hildie's brother?"

"Oh, yeah. That one was a little looker."

"Now he's a big looker."

"And this is a problem because . . ."

"He's a totally egotistical jerk."

"Really?" She narrows her eyes at me. "He always seemed like a pretty nice kid."

"Well, he's not. He's insensitive and overprivileged, and I hate him."

"Methinks thou doth protest too much."

"Shutteth uppeth."

"Okay." I expect her to hang on to this topic like a pit bull on angel dust, but instead she takes a deep breath as if she needs to calm herself down. Ever since she started yoga, she's always doing this fancy breathing. She says she has to feed her mind plenty of oxygen to stave off Alzheimer's. She's not getting Alzheimer's — she just likes thinking about illness. It's like a hobby with her.

"So what's your blood pressure, Aunt Ann?"

"One oh four over eighty," she says with great pride as she finally sits down in a chair like a normal person. "I've been drinking plenty of water," she says, and then takes another deep breath. I'm starting to suspect that this is more than the usual health-obsessed breathing, because she's studying me warily.

"What's up?"

"Oh . . ." she says nervously. I can tell from her thoughts that whatever she has to say involves my dad and it's big. "Well, honey," she says, "your dad called today. Just now. I just got off the phone with him."

"Uh-huh."

She takes a deep breath and holds it. Her cheeks puff out, giving her narrow face the shape of a butternut squash. "He's coming home for a visit," she finally blurts.

I have stopped breathing. Every muscle in my body is clenched as though I could squeeze myself calm. Except that I am calm, but I don't *think* I'm calm. I feel my mouth open, and I think I should use it to say something, but instead all I can do is look at Minnie Mouse, who has curled into the shape of a cinnamon bun on the bottom shelf of our bookcase. She's watching me with her yellow eyes.

Her eyes suddenly look spooky and alien to me.

Her creepy yellow eyes are freaking me out.

Everything is freaking me out.

"Before you freak, honey"—Aunt Ann takes hold of my fingers and squeezes them with a sweaty hand—"let me tell you that he regrets leaving the way he did more than anything in his life, and he's ashamed of himself, and he feels like he's really let you down. He hasn't had the courage to come home until now, but he really wants to try and reconnect with you because you're so important to him."

"Uh-huh," I say, trying to work out how much of this came from Dad and how much is Aunt Ann's *interpretation* of what came from him. Dad doesn't use words like *ashamed* or *reconnect*.

"He's flying back next week. And I need to know—do you want to come to the airport with me?" She grinds her little teeth together and raises her eyebrows.

I'm silent, waiting for someone to speak. But the only person who can answer the question is me, so I say, "Um . . ."

"I think you should, Kristi, honey." She glances at the door because she hears a car door slam and she's afraid it might be Mom. "I really think you need to show him that you're ready to forgive him."

I do? I am?

"So his flight is next Thursday evening at seven thirty-eight, but let's get there a little early because those parking garages are so big, and then we'll both be at security waiting for him, and we'll be holding hands."

"Uh . . ." I get a mental flash of us standing near the metal detectors in the airport, and I realize this is Aunt Ann's fantasy of how I will be there to comfort *her* when her baby brother comes back to America after two years of fighting horrific African diseases.

"I hope he's not *carrying* anything," she says as she scoots off the chair and stands up. "I'm sure they get shots, but Jesus, some of the diseases they have there are —" She roots through her purse, looking for her hand sanitizer. "I think I'll look into getting us some shots beforehand. We could just get all those shots you're supposed to get before going to Africa and that way we'll be safe."

"I don't like shots," I say.

"Nonsense, honey. It's a tiny little needle and your skin is so big!"

Suddenly I'm trying to breathe all the air in the room at once. Aunt Ann stops looking for her sanitizer and sits next to me, her hand on my back. She rubs and rubs. She stays until I can breathe normally, but leaves soon after because it's dark outside and she doesn't want to be here when Mom finds out. Dad's coming home.

TELLING MOM

By the time Mom gets home I am calmly watching news footage of a terrible bus crash. When Minnie hears the garage door she jumps off the couch and pads back to my room. I follow her and lock the padlock. Who says you can't train cats?

I wish I could train her to tell Mom about Dad coming home.

Mom comes in breathless. "Hi, honey!" She smiles at me, something in her expression unfamiliar. She's different. I can't put my finger on it until she stretches her arms over her head, saying, "It's weird sitting down most of the day!"

Oh. That's what's different. She's not exhausted.

Instead of her usual scrubs she's wearing a nice skirt, stockings, blue leather pumps, and a silk blazer. She looks skinnier. Somehow the skirt hides her thick legs and the blazer shapes itself to her waistline. Her eyes look really huge and black because she has actually put on makeup. She never used to wear makeup because she says it can interfere with the sterile environment of the operating room. She's even wearing lipstick, so her lips look a lot fuller than usual. She looks good. She almost looks pretty. Suddenly I see why people expect me to take it as a compliment when they say I look just like my mother. Maybe to them, it is.

"Did you order dinner?" she asks.

I shake my head no. For the first time in over two years, I feel like wrapping my arms around her neck and letting her hug me. But I haven't let her hug me in a long time and I'm not about to start now. She stands in the hallway pulling off her shoes and then her stockings, and then she walks into the bathroom calling over her shoulder, "What do you feel like tonight? How about steamed Chinese vegetables? Or I hear there's a new Indian place that delivers. We can do that, as long as you don't order anything too greasy."

"Dad's coming home," I say.

I wait, standing in the living room. She slowly comes back out of the bathroom, one hand frozen in the process of pulling pins from her hair. She drops her hand and her hair twirls into a curl and rests on her shoulder as though it is suddenly overcome with emotion. Her oval face becomes very sharp. "What?" she says, despite the fact that her voice has cracked down the middle.

"Dad's coming home. Next Thursday."

She stares at me, her lip hanging to show her bottom teeth. "How do you know?"

"Aunt Ann came by."

"Well, he's not staying here."

I remember what Aunt Ann said, and I panic. "But we have

to show him we forgive him so that he won't be afraid of us and he'll stay!"

Mom's dark eyes travel my face. There is such pity in the way she looks at me, I don't even have to read her mind to know she's thinking, *Poor Kristi.* But thinking this only seems to make her angrier. Slowly she walks to the couch and sits down, her fingers pushing at her temples, rubbing, rubbing. She closes her eyes and breathes in through her nose and out through her mouth, but this seems to make her feel weak, and she bends over to hold her head between her knees like you're supposed to do if you feel like passing out.

She stays like that a long time, then straightens back up and grabs the phone. As she dials she pats the cushion next to her. I tiptoe over and sit by her, which is quite unlike me, but I feel like we're in battle conditions and the couch is our foxhole. I swear, I even smell smoke.

"Hello, Ann?" Mom says. "Yes, Kristi just told me . . . No, I'm not mad. I just need to know his plans . . . Of course this isn't your fault—we're all just doing the best we can . . . Ann, I need you to calm down for a second and just focus, okay? . . . Is he staying with you? . . . Well, can he? Because I'm just not ready to have him— . . . I see. Okay . . . Yes . . . Only if *Kristi* wants to. I don't want anyone talking her into anything, do you understand me? . . . Ann, no matter what you do, things will take their natural course . . . Well, at this point, I don't know what to hope for."

Listening to their conversation is like listening to bombs

going off, one by one. With each explosion the sound gets closer and closer. There is so much noise in my mind, I can't tell if the bombs are in my thoughts or in Mom's. Maybe they're in both.

I desperately want to go find my earphones and put on Maria Callas at full volume, but I can't make myself get off the couch.

I barely notice when Mom hangs up and puts her arms around me.

I don't even care that she's squishing my face into her armpit.

We sit like that until our stomachs rumble, and then we fix organic peanut butter and jelly sandwiches and watch the end of *Terminator 2: Judgment Day,* and then we drive to the all-night market and buy two pints of all-natural ice cream, strawberry for her and double fudge chocolate chip for me, and we each eat an entire pint in the car, and then we come back home and realize that somehow we're still hungry but all we have is whole-wheat bread and organic goat cheese she bought at the farmers' market, so we fry up grilled cheese sandwiches, and they're crispy and salty and comforting somehow. We don't talk about Dad or Aunt Ann or anything. We barely talk at all. We watch the news until we are both so exhausted that we can't keep our eyes open. I fall asleep on the couch, and she falls asleep on the recliner. In the morning we both feel completely ill, and we look like someone parked a Sherman tank on our faces, our hair sticking up in every direction. Mom goes to the shower, but she doesn't sing at all. Usually she sings. I go to my room and take my daily bubble bath, but I don't break down and I don't cry.

I'm glad I don't cry. But I don't know why I don't. It seems strange to me.

WREAKING HAVOC WITH MALLORY

Today is Friday, and that means we have Processing during the last few minutes of school. It's a bizarre ritual that entails people saying whatever is on their minds, and everyone in the school is supposed to listen with an open heart. If I possibly could, I would keep my earphones on, but Betty Pasternak is sitting right behind me and she expects me to listen.

Gusty is sitting across the room from me with his legs crossed and his elbows on his knees. I try to search his thoughts to see if he's still mad at me, though I'm not completely sure what I did to make him mad, unless the "impervious to false flattery" thing was insulting or something. Evil Incarnate is whispering at him and he nods, but he seems to be looking for someone, because his eyes are trailing along the crowd. When he sees me, his eyes stop and he kind of straightens up. I know I should look away, I really should, but I can't stop looking at him. He doesn't seem mad. But he doesn't seem happy. Or neutral. I listen for his thoughts but there's so much else happening in the room that I can't get a read on him.

Finally he tilts his head to one side and raises his hand in a kind of wave. I nod at him. By now Evil has found who he is looking at, and her eyes fix on me with dark hatred. I look away. Sometimes I just don't have the energy to return the nastiness I receive. Especially knowing that my dad is coming back in six days after being gone for two whole years. This thought alone drains me of energy, leaving barely enough to keep my heart beating.

Brian walks to the center of the circle, the usual seething smile on his weirdly wide face. Today he is holding a big yellow bell, and he swings it in an arc. It makes a rude clanging noise, and everyone stops to look. Once the room is quiet Brian laughs and says, "Do you like my new bell? This is the attention bell, and from now on, when you hear it, that means it's time for our meetings to begin, okay?"

"Okay," Jacob Flax says.

Some people snigger. Gusty doesn't, though.

"Who wants to start off this week's Processing session?"

Gusty raises his hand, but Brian doesn't see him and calls on one of the guys on our lacrosse team instead. The guy stands up and announces, "I think our fall dance should be a costume party this year, and we should have it on Halloween since it falls on a Friday anyway."

Brian raises his eyebrows as if this were the most brilliant idea since Newton discovered gravity. "Okay, I like it. Are there countersuggestions?"

A girl with long black hair and light blond roots raises her hand. "I think everyone should come as vampires!"

The whole room erupts into a million pointless conversations about the pointless Halloween dance, and Brian starts ringing the bell as if he were calling the entire solar system to attention. "Calm down, everyone! Let's put it to the ballot box and we'll vote on it, okay?"

This shuts everyone up.

"Does anyone have anything else to share?"

Gusty raises his hand again and this time Brian sees him. "Gusty, what's on your mind?"

Gusty stands up. He has one hand in the back pocket of his jeans, and he's hunched over, embarrassed. "Uh, there's someone I just want to apologize to. For some stuff. And maybe we can talk about it later. I just want to say I didn't act very—um—mature and that next time we get together I hope it'll go better."

He sits back down and doesn't exactly glance at me, but his eyes definitely dart in my direction. His thoughts float over to me, gently, and the word, *Okay?* drops onto me like a fluffy white feather.

Yes, he's too gorgeous for his own good, but he's trying to be nice. I look at him until our eyes find each other, and I give him a little smile. He smiles, too, which makes him look simply dazzling.

"Thank you, Gusty." Brian clears his throat. "I hope everyone has gotten a chance to welcome Mallory to our school." With a curl of his wrist he beckons Mallory to the center of the circle. Mallory strides over to stand next to him, his face turning an even brighter red. He hates this. Why does Brian have to single people out? "If you haven't said hello to Mallory, please do. I'm sure he'd like to hear from you." He raises his eyebrows at Mallory. "Do you want to add anything to what I've said, Mallory?"

"Rock on," Mallory says, and then walks back to the perimeter of the room.

The end of Processing is always the same. We have to sing our school song, which is so boring and stupid that I won't bother with the lyrics. Here's a quick paraphrase: *Journeys is great. Freedom lives on. Get to know yourself. Nature nature blah blah. We are all special. Until we meet again. Now let's all go and pick our butts and think about how great our crusty anuses are. Until we meet again.*

We all head for the doors, and I'm looking for Gusty because maybe he wants to talk right now, but Mallory catches up with me. "Hey, Kristi, want to come hang out at my house?" I can feel him thinking, *Don't look at her boobs. Don't look at her boobs. Don't look*—but he can't help it. He slops up a huge eyeful. I wait for his eyes to travel back to my face. It takes a very uncomfortable amount of time.

"Uh . . ." I look through the crowd in time to see that Gusty has just rushed out the front door. I hear his skateboard slap the sidewalk and it speeds away. I try to catch my mind up to him, but he and his thoughts are out of reach.

"Ground control to Major Kristi, do you read?" I see Mallory is looking at me with a dopey grin. "Want to come over?"

I feel my chin tense up the way it does just before I start to cry, but that is obviously the last thing I would ever do over Gusty Peterson. He is a beautiful person, and he is apt to say one thing and do another. Not to be trusted. Beautiful people = BAD.

"I have a better idea," I tell Mallory, and I head for the park.

I walk fast, forcing Gusty and his weird apology out of my mind. I don't need to think about Gusty Peterson because Gusty Peterson doesn't matter to me. He just doesn't.

It's late September by now, and the sun feels farther away. The wind ebbs and flows, and already leaves are collecting at the edges of the schoolyard. As we walk, Mallory has one hand crammed into the hip pocket of his white hemp jeans, and with the other he smokes, jabbing his cigarette between his lips and taking short, violent puffs on it. Something about the way he moves, even the way he holds still, reminds me of a coiled spring, as if a light touch in just the right place could send him bouncing out of control. I like this about him because I feel the same spring inside of me, and I long for someone to come along and trip my wire.

It's better to be with Mallory. He doesn't think I'm sick like Gusty does. I have no reason to think about Gusty. I'm not thinking about Gusty and the way he left without talking to me. Unless —

Of course. I'm so stupid! He wasn't talking to me during Processing at all! How could I be so dense?

But he smiled at me right after. He smiled as though we understood each other.

But then he left without talking to me. He just ran away.

I'm not going to think about this. That's it. I'm through thinking about him.

I mean it.

"So what do you want to do?" Mallory asks me.

"Do you enjoy wreaking havoc?"

"Havoc is my favorite pastime, second only to wreaking."

"Then this is the beginning of a beautiful friendship."

I lead Mallory to the edge of the Journeys parking lot, where I scoop up a whole lot of the sand and dust that collect near the wall of the school building. I can feel the grit working its way underneath my fingernails. I'm usually a clean person, but I like this feeling anyway. Dirt always feels comforting.

"What are you going to use that for?" Mallory asks me.

"You'll see," I tell him as I slip several handfuls into a plastic bag from a nearby trash can.

I take him down Conway Street because it's lined with huge cottonwood trees and I love the sound of the wind moving through them. I make my mind quiet, and I can feel Mallory's mind is quiet, too, so I don't need my opera. Relaxing is usually the last thing I can do with another person around, and it makes me glad that Mallory moved to our school, because I can sort of relax with him.

Then I feel him thinking about my plump, naked body, and I get a little grossed out.

"So I guess Eva Kearns-Tate is your character ed partner?" I say, to distract him from his lurid thoughts.

"Yeah, she seems cool."

"Just wait," I tell him. "She has a nasty streak."

"Really?" He lowers his eyebrows. "She was really sweet to me."

Everyone thinks Eva is nice because they can't hear her thoughts. She was probably thinking nothing but horrible things about Mallory, and he was blissfully shielded.

We turn the corner and the park comes into view. There's a really strong breeze, so my practical joke should go just fine as long as I'm careful. This one is much more difficult to execute because it relies on a lot of variables. I lead Mallory over to a bench that is perfectly placed behind a big bush. From the path we can't be seen, though we can get little peeks at passersby through the spaces between the leaves. Once they get past the bush, they're in full view. To give Mallory a good show, I'll have to time this very carefully.

"So what do we do?" he asks me, his eyes on the bag of sand I've set between us on the bench.

"First we do a few test runs." I check the direction of the wind, which is at our backs, and then I pour a little sand into the palm of my hand.

"What the hell?" Mallory asks.

"Shush," I tell him as I toss the sand to see where the wind takes it. It flies right into the bush at about knee level. Not high enough. I pour more sand into my hand, and when the wind picks up, I toss it as high as it will go. This gives the sand a better trajectory.

"Dude. What the hell are you doing?"

"Shush," I tell him again as I watch the sand and dust float through the bush to the bike path in a sheer brown cloud. "Perfect," I say.

"Okay . . ." Mallory says, adding about four extra syllables to the *kay* to indicate he is questioning my sanity. "What next? Do we pour the sand in our shoes?"

"We wait. And watch."

We have to wait for a long time and I'm about to decide it isn't going to work, but then in the distance I see a woman running in baggy little shorts. Quickly I grab two big handfuls of sand, then nod at Mallory as though we are deep in conversation and he has just said something very witty. "You said it!" I tell him. "He totally did!"

He looks at me with sincere concern.

I peek over my shoulder at my target.

I can catch flickers of her through the leaves. She's puffing along, in her own world, humming a little to herself. The wind gets particularly fierce when she is about to hit the sweet spot.

I toss the sand into the air, one handful and then the other. It becomes a tornado of filth moving at about thirty miles an hour over the bush. The dust cloud drifts right where I want it to and hits her in the face just as she's coming into full view.

She sputters, squeezing her eyes shut, then trips over her own feet and falls hard onto the pavement. "Oh! Ah!" she cries as she rolls on the ground, hugging her knee.

She's hurt.

"Oh, no," I say, but Mallory falls off the bench laughing.

I've been doing this for a long time, but this is my first real casualty. I rush over to help her. When I get close up, I see that a layer of skin has been peeled from her knee, leaving an oozing red patch. It's so gross that I have to take a deep breath. A little sand in the face is one thing, but I didn't want to hurt anyone. Usually they just sneeze.

She blows on the wound as a tear slides down her cheek. She'd looked like a college student from far away, but now I can see she has deep wrinkles around her eyes.

"Are you okay?" I ask, kneeling beside her.

"I think so," she says, but her voice sounds like it's being forced through a tight opening. Her eyes are watering like crazy from all the sand, but I can tell her knee hurts so bad that she doesn't even care about her eyes.

"Can you stand up?" I ask.

"Give me a minute."

While I wait for her to catch her breath, I glare at Mallory, who is still giggling.

When the woman stops shaking, she nods at me and I hold out my hand. We hook fists, and I pull her up. She wobbles at first, and once she has her balance she gingerly tries to put weight on her knee. "It's okay, I think."

"Can you walk home?"

"Yeah. You're such a sweetie, uh . . ."

"Mindy Nightingale."

I catch her thinking, *What a cutie pie!* And I feel even worse.

"Well, you're a lifesaver, Mindy," she says before glaring at Mallory, who, upon hearing my alias, has turned magenta from laughter and is convulsing spastically.

After she limps away, Mallory cannot stop talking about how cool that was. "You are a master! I mean, I've seen mischief in my time, but that was a work of art! You timed it all perfectly!" He pulls a cigarette out and lights it, his face aglow with admiration. "How did you know it would hit her in the face like that?"

"Months of experimentation." I'm still cringing inside, thinking about her skinned knee, but I can't help feeling happy that Mallory appreciates my gift for evildoing.

Still, seeing the way Mallory laughed at someone getting hurt makes me realize there's something a little ugly about that kind of laughter. Am I that mean, really, that I enjoy hurting other people? Do I *want* to be that mean?

It occurs to me that Gusty wouldn't have laughed at the woman falling down. Gusty would have helped her.

But I'm not thinking about Gusty Peterson anymore.

JACOB FLAX IS ATTRACTIVE

My weekend is totally sans fun. Mom digs up some carrots from her wormy garden and makes me eat carrot ginger soup, which is infinitely less satisfying than a meatiest, treatiest pizza. It's a little nerve-racking, spending so much time at home with Mom. Now that she's working a nine-to-five job, I figure that one of these days she and Minnie are going to cross paths, and I really don't know what I'm going to do when that happens.

I spend a lot of time sewing up a new gypsy skirt patched together from surgical scrubs Dad left behind. Melon and mint green go surprisingly well together, and the skirt will look fabulous with the rag shirt I wove together from strips of green curtains. On top I'm all texture, and on the bottom I'm all pattern. I'm getting good at sewing. My new outfit looks like something I picked up at a couture boutique.

It's a very complicated project, so I don't have time to think about Gusty Peterson at all. Well, I think a little bit about how proud I am that I'm not thinking about him. But that's it.

Sunday night I try on my new outfit, and Minnie purrs really loud, so I can tell she loves it.

So Monday morning comes, and I wake up with my usual lust for life, which is none. I lie in bed a little too long so that by the time I roll down my laundry-pile exit ramp, it's 6:45 and I only have time to take a quick cat bath. "Am I doing this right?" I ask Minnie, and she crinkles up her yellow eyes and vibes me with adoration from the edge of my tub.

I skip washing my hair and have to sacrifice·the third layer of eyeliner, so my eyes don't look nearly dark and mysterious enough, but that's the breaks. I hurry out the door with barely enough time to fill up my travel mug. Mom calls after me from her bathroom, "I'll see you tonight, Kristi!"

"Okay!" I yell. Ever since I found out Dad's coming home, it's easier to be nice to Mom. I don't know why.

The walk to school is normal. I'm listening to *Madame Butterfly* today and that puts me in a good mood. For some reason all the best operas end in suicide — don't ask me why. Jacob catches up with me at the corner and prattles on. I'm so used to him trailing after me that I barely look at him until Felix Mathers, the cadaverous musical genius who plays nine instruments, yells from behind us, "Hey, Jacob, looking good!" When I glance back at Felix, he tucks in his chin and doubles his pace. He is one weird dude.

I finally turn to look at Jacob and am completely shocked by what I see.

Jacob Flax got a tan.

"What the hell?" I say to him as I lurch to a halt and yank off my headphones.

"You like?" he asks. His skin is the perfect shade of pale brown, which brings out his white-blue eyes. He smiles at me, and I can see that already the gaps between his teeth are starting to close. His hair has yellow tips that brighten up everything about him, and he's put just enough gel in it so that it lifts off his forehead in perfect messy curls.

He is completely transformed. I am so shocked that black spots crowd my vision and I have to take deep breaths.

Jacob Flax is . . . attractive.

"You're . . ." I pause, because I don't really want to say it, but somehow I can't help myself. ". . . *attractive!* What the hell did you *do?*"

He is so thrilled, his cheeks turn a beautiful shade of blushy peach. His teeth positively glisten. "I got my new set of invisible braces so my teeth look better. And I had my hair highlighted, and I got some of that self-tanning cream, but I'm also going to the tanning booth, so pretty soon the color will be real. Cool, eh?"

My entire sense of reality will need to be revamped, from my base assumptions about physical matter to my understanding of evolutionary theory. Jacob Flax is not supposed to be attractive. It just isn't appropriate.

"But—"

"Also, Abercrombie and Fitch had a sale." He twirls around, and I realize that his pale blue T-shirt, which matches his eyes beautifully, clings to what I can only describe as muscles on his chest and arms. Small muscles, but they're there. He smiles gleefully. "So I guess taking charge of my life is kind of paying off, huh?"

"Yeah," I say.

"Hey, nice outfit," he says. Jacob's eyes travel down my breasts and then over my new patchwork skirt. "I think this is your best work yet."

"Thanks," I say, but I turn away and start walking to school because I get an image of myself in a string bikini. For the first time I'm not grossed out by Jacob picturing my boobs. And that disturbs me.

"Anyway, now that I'm attractive, I have something very important to talk to you about, Kristi."

"Oh, no, Jacob. I can't," I say, because I know what's coming. He wants to take me out. He wants to slobber all over me. He wants to rub his skinny body on my fat body. "I'm kind of overloaded right now."

My voice wavers a little bit, and that's enough for Jacob to jump all over it. "Why? What's up? Are you okay?"

Normally I wouldn't tell him a single private thing about me, but I'm desperate to make him stop imagining rubbing my boobs with tanning oil. "My dad is coming back on Thursday and I'm kind of freaked out."

"Wow, Kristi." He grabs my arm and turns me toward him. We're almost at the school building, and we're right under the pink tree, standing on a carpet of pink flowers. "That's super serious."

I am suddenly distracted by the fact that Jacob has said two s-words and I'm completely dry. "You're not spitting."

"I figured out I should swallow before I talk. Aren't you freaked out about your dad?" He is so concerned that I feel the need to walk away from him.

Concern from others is the last kind of vibe I can cope with. Concern makes me feel sorry for myself, and then I just start crying, and then people want to comfort me, and I really hate that. A lot. "Yeah," I say, "but it's no big deal. I'm over all that."

"But he's your parent, and he left you right when you started going through puberty! I mean, it's like you're a whole different person now, and he doesn't know you at all!"

"My Aunt Ann has sent him pictures," I say as I grind my toe into pink flower petals to see if they'll bruise.

"Stop trivializing this!" He's so exasperated that he spits all over me.

"Swallow, Jacob," I say as I wipe off my neck.

"Sorry." We walk across the schoolyard toward the building. He lets his shoulder touch mine every few steps, which is as close to hugging as I ever want to get with him. However attractive he is, he is still Jacob Flax. To prove he is still Jacob Flax, he begins talking again in his squeaky voice. "Anyway, I understand that you're feeling overloaded, but I wanted to ask you about Gusty, since he's your character education partner. He seems like a nice person to socialize with. Not stuck-up at all."

"No one that gorgeous could be humble, Jacob." I guess

now that Jacob isn't an eyesore, he hopes to join the ranks of the cool. More power to him, I guess.

"Since you know him better than I do, how would you suggest I approach him to ask if he wants to socialize?"

"I don't know, Jacob, but don't say 'socialize.' Ask if he wants to hang out."

"Hang out. Got it. You don't need to mention this to Mallory," Jacob says just before we get to the door. People are flowing past us into the building. As one senior girl rushes by, I hear her thinking, *Beauty and the beast.* I'm not Beauty. Jacob gives my arm a little shake and I look into his eyes, which are dancing nervously. "I'm not sure Mallory is a very friendly person, and I would appreciate it if you did not discuss my personal matters with him."

As if gossip about Jacob were a social currency I could ever use. "I won't."

"And, Kristi." He rubs his hand up and down my arm. His mouth is twisted into a sympathetic half smile. "If you need to talk about your dad, just tell me, okay?"

"Jacob, chill, please. I'm okay." I put on my headphones, turn up the volume, and walk into Journeys.

I hover through the morning like a butterfly in a gravity-free environment. Nothing touches me. In Explorations of Nature we've reached the reproduction unit, and David has brought in these huge orange stargazer lilies for us to stare at while he lectures about stamens and pistils and pollen and bees and crap. Hildie keeps raising her hand and asking him to repeat himself, and at one point he rushes over to show her how to spell *pollination*. She leans toward the table, and he leans closer to her. Martin Jacobson sniggers, and that makes David straighten up quickly, stroking his black goatee. He gives us each a list of vocabulary words and assigns us a free-verse contemplation about the role of the wind in the reproduction of flowering plants.

We all file to the Contemplation Room and I find a table that I can have all to myself. Here's my poem:

> *Oh, wind, I love the way you rub pollen on my pistil.*
> *Your sweet caress really gets my nectar flowing.*
> *You can pollinate me anytime you want.*
> *Pollinate me from behind*
> *Or face to face.*
> *Pollinate me in the middle of the night*
> *Or in the morning before work.*
> *I don't care if you stalk me or stem me,*
> *Just make sure you put your metal to my petal,*
> *Gusty, lusty wind.*

I write the entire last line before I realize that somehow Gusty's name snuck into my poem. Gusty's name doesn't belong in anything I think or write. I erase it so hard that I wear through the paper. That was totally, completely, absolutely an accident. That's all. Accident. Chance. It has nothing to do with Gusty Peterson.

I close my eyes and hold my breath until I can clear my mind completely. I have Charlotte Church's flawless tones blaring in my brain, and I concentrate on her soprano and let her soothe me. She has finished one aria and begun another by the time I feel almost totally normal. I am calm enough now to maybe work on another Gusty-free verse for Explorations of Nature.

I open my eyes and who do I see sitting across from me? Gusty Peterson. Naturally.

I smell the peppermint and leather, his unique scent I can't help liking. He's biting his lower lip as his green eyes flutter over me. He smiles tentatively.

I cannot report what expression is on my face — that's how surprised I am.

He slides a piece of paper toward me and raises his golden eyebrows. I look down to see the words *I'm sorry about the way I acted.*

My face must be asking some kind of question, because he takes the paper back and writes, *I got really embarrassed during our last meeting, and I don't deal well in situations like that. And then I made that announcement at Processing last week and I wanted to talk, but then you were talking to Mallory.*

His expression is confusing to me. He doesn't seem able to lift his eyes high enough to look at my face, but he isn't looking at my breasts, either. I think he's looking at my hands, and that makes me glad that I filed my nails and painted them pink this weekend. I could turn down Charlotte Church so that I can hear his thoughts, but somehow I don't want to. I want to pretend I'm not an overplump psychic with ginormous gazungas talking to a supernaturally good-looking egomaniac. It feels nice to pretend we're two regular people sitting in an irregular school. It's like a vacation from the inside of my head.

Hesitantly, he writes something more on the paper and slides it over to me. *I was thinking it might be fun to do our next character ed assignment at Pluribus after school today. We could get some grindage.*

Assuming that *grindage* means food and not human body parts, I nod at him. I'm terrified and happy at once. All that emotion crashes through my body and ends up at my eyes, forcing tears that I can barely fight back. How freakish would I have to be to start *crying* now? And anyway, what is my problem? Grindage. What the hell is cathartic about *that*?

He doesn't seem to notice anything. He breaks into a blinding smile and gets up to go. Before he leaves, though, he lifts aside one of my headphones and whispers into my ear, "I'll meet you at the pink tree."

I can still feel his breath on my cheek, even after he has left the room.

GUSTY'S LIFE AS A DOG

I am standing under the pink tree, waiting for Gusty and noticing the way the sunlight makes the petals on the flowers turn a warm peach color. I also notice for the first time the glowing, fresh scent of this tree. It's an amazing fragrance that makes me think of a delicious fruit that would be too beautiful to eat. My feet are surrounded by a thick layer of pink petals. I kick into them until my toes are completely covered and imagine that the ground is made of nothing but pink petals all the way to the earth's core.

Gusty walks out of the school building and comes toward me. He's carrying his skateboard under his arm, and he has a huge satchel slung over his shoulder. He smiles. My stomach tumbles and I have to take deep breaths.

"Hey," he says.

"Hey."

We stand looking uncomfortable for a second before he tosses his head in the direction of Pluribus. I follow him.

We walk quietly next to each other. My mind is buzzing, so I can't get a read on his thoughts, but that's just the way I like it. I don't want to know what he's thinking. I should protect myself better, but I can't help feeling happy.

We are walking along a tree-lined sidewalk when we see a dog zigzagging down the road. He is brown with white speckles, and he has the kind of retarded smile on his face only dogs can muster. If he's not careful he'll get picked up by the dogcatcher.

Gusty grins. "Someone's on a joy ride."

The dog pauses for a second to look at us, his head slightly cocked. He seems to be wondering if we're going to turn him in. Without a word, Gusty sets his skateboard and book bag onto the sidewalk. He trots toward the dog. "What are you doing?" I ask him, but he doesn't answer. The dog seems to understand him perfectly, and he jumps into the air with a surge of doggy joy. Gusty laughs and starts rubbing the dog's ears. The dog loves this so much, he rams his head into Gusty's knees, which makes Gusty lose his balance and fall down on someone's lawn. The second he's down, the dog starts licking Gusty's face ferociously.

This is some kind of primordial ritual I do not understand. "Do you guys need to be alone?" I ask.

Gusty laughs. "No! I'm just happy."

"Is that your dog?" I ask him.

Gusty looks at me quizzically. "Huh? No." They're both out of breath and panting. He lays his head on the dog's back, and the dog curls his head around and sniffs Gusty's neck before giving him a disturbingly sensual kiss.

"Tell me you *know* this dog. Please."

"We've never met." He gives the dog a good rub on the flank before getting up and brushing fur off himself. The dog licks the palm of Gusty's hand.

"Are you sure that's safe?" I ask him. "What if he has some kind of disease?"

He seems amused by this. "He's a perfectly healthy animal."

"Okay."

"Come pet him."

Looking at the dog's big white teeth, I say, "I only like animals that can't kill me."

"He wouldn't hurt a fly." He kneels down and holds the dog's face toward me. The dog's huge pink tongue flops over Gusty's hand, and I wonder how Gusty can stand the slobber. Slobber is one of many reasons why I am a cat person. "Pet him."

"Em . . ." I look at him, nervous.

"Come on!" He reaches a hand toward me.

I put my backpack on Gusty's skateboard and kneel on the grass next to them. The dog kicks one paw out and it lands on my new skirt. Praying he doesn't have poop between his toes, I slowly, slowly reach my hand toward his head. I give him two little pats and pull away.

"That's not enough. Really rub him, like this." Gusty takes hold of the dog's ear and massages it. One side of the dog's body seems to melt. "Now you," Gusty says, and takes hold of my wrist.

Because I love the way Gusty's thumb moves over my skin

as if he can't resist feeling the friction between us, I take hold of the dog's ear and rub it the way Gusty did. The dog stiffens at first because I'm not doing it right, but then I realize he isn't that different from Minnie, who has this special spot right where her ear meets her skull. So I find that spot on the dog and I start to really rub. He melts for me just the way he melted for Gusty, and he lifts his eyes to look into mine. It's funny, because I love the way Minnie looks at me, her yellow eyes so warm and loving, but this dog's eyes remind me of a person's eyes. They're round, with round pupils, not the narrow pupils that Minnie has. Something about the dog feels a little human, and that makes me realize why I was never a dog person. I hate humans. Most humans.

I look up, and Gusty is watching me as if I am completely fascinating. Just looking. Looking at me. I listen to his thoughts, but I don't hear words. I get only a feeling of warmth from them, like sunlight.

My face gets hot, and I turn toward the dog so Gusty can't see me blushing. I start rubbing the dog's other ear so he gets a double whammy, and I go in for a really deep rub, but my thumb grazes something sharp in his fur. Suddenly the dog yelps, leaps away, and snaps at my hand in one motion.

"Oh my God!" I yell.

Gusty grabs the dog and holds its head to his chest to keep him still. "What happened?"

"He tried to bite me!" I feel betrayed. I look at the dog, who is whining softly as if he's trying to whisper to Gusty.

"Did he get you?"

"No, but he tried."

"Kristi, dogs don't *try* to bite. If he meant to bite you, you'd have gotten bit. He's telling you to keep away from that spot because it hurts him. That's all."

I still feel totally rejected. By a dog.

"Did you rub him too hard?" Gusty asks as he examines the dog's face.

"I felt something sharp in his ear." I point to the dog's left ear, and Gusty lifts it up, speaking in a very gentle voice.

"It's okay, boy—let's just check this out." He runs his fingers through the hair under the dog's ears, and the dog jerks his head as though he wants to bite Gusty and whines. "That's it!" Gusty pinches something just inside the dog's ear and pulls it out. It comes with a whole lot of fur. "He had a nasty bur in his ear, and you must have pushed on it and really hurt him."

"I'm sorry."

"It's not your fault." Gusty smiles at me as he flicks the bur away. "Here." He pulls on my wrist again. I don't want to, but then the dog licks my hand, looking at me sideways with his big brown eyes. "See? He still wants to be friends," Gusty says, and chuckles. "He's a cute dog."

I smile. The dog forgives me for hurting him. I'm not sure whether I should respect him for that or feel sorry for him. With an attitude like that, he's a sitting duck.

Gusty stands and picks up everything we left on the curb. He slings his satchel over one shoulder and my pack over the other. "Let's get going," he says, and we start off again toward Pluribus. The dog follows for a few minutes, but then gives Gusty's hand a last lick before turning to go down a different street. I watch him go, but Gusty doesn't even give him a second glance.

"So, what's that all about?" I ask Gusty.

"What?"

"Your freakish affinity with canines."

"Oh." He shrugs. "I don't know. I've just always understood them."

"What is there to understand?"

"A lot. Body language, vocalization, facial expression, behavior. Even as a kid I could tell by looking if a dog was friendly or mean, scared or happy. They're just easy to me, easier than people. Cats, too, though they're different."

"Yeah, they are."

"I think dogs like me because they can tell I like them. And sometimes they just seem relieved to meet a person who understands them."

"I can understand that," I say. I never knew Gusty had a deep side. I always thought he was dumb in proportion to his looks. Maybe I wanted to believe he was dumb because I thought he didn't like me. The truth is, he never really seemed dumb. Not really. And even if he does think I'm sick, that doesn't mean we can't be friends, right? I'm kind of friends with Jacob, even though I find his spitting problem rather disgusting. So Gusty thinking I'm sick isn't *necessarily* so terrible, right? Maybe he thinks I'm sick like a cool mad scientist kind of person. Or maybe he thinks I'm crazy in a fascinating way like Carmen, in the opera by Bizet.

"Understanding is rare," Gusty says, and I figure he's still thinking about dogs while I'm working my brain trying to figure him out.

"Truer words were never spoken," I say. And we're silent the rest of the way to Pluribus.

PLURIBUS

Pluribus is the coolest place in our town. All the windows are stained glass, and the ceiling is super high with lots of rough-hewed beams and rafters. Tons of plants hang everywhere, getting their light from the skylights in the ceiling. I hardly ever come here even though I really like it because this is where all the kids from Journeys hang out and I'm usually avoiding them.

Gusty and I are halfway through the nachos before he finally pages through his notebook for our character education assignment. "Okay. We have to list our greatest liabilities now."

I take a long swallow of my root beer while I absorb this information. The last thing I want to tell Gusty about is my dark side. "How do you always know what we're supposed to do for character education?" I ask as a way to keep the subject impersonal.

"The bulletin board. Where we found out who our partners were? Don't you check it?"

"No."

"I'll go first, okay? This shouldn't be too hard." He pulls a pen out of the spine of one of his notebooks. "Me. Hmm. Well, I'm not very good at schoolwork. I get too bored. I let my teachers think I'm slow because then they don't expect much from me and they leave me alone."

"Good strategy," I tell him. I honestly admire him for this. He's an underachiever, but he's very good at it. My opinion of his smarts just shot up like ten points.

"I should try harder, but I'd rather read about things I find interesting, like animal behavior and ecology. I like marine biology, too. Shark behavior. Stuff like that."

"Got it." I take the pen from him and start writing. "What else?"

"I'm shy, so I'm not very good at confrontation. My sense of humor is really zany, so most people don't get it and they just act embarrassed for me. Also, I don't have the greatest table manners, my mom says. My room is really messy because I never fold my laundry until it sits on my bed for about five days and gets all wrinkly. Also, I skateboard with a total disregard for human life. My own, mostly. How many is that?"

"Six."

"Okay. I'm mean to my sister sometimes. And I hate my mom. I shouldn't, but I think she's really selfish. She won't let me have a dog, and she ignores everything my dad says because she makes more money than him, and she's bitter about being the breadwinner. So I just ignore her, which is probably why I'm bad at confrontation. Let's see. Oh, I'm lazy. Lazy in my mind. Not my body. Is that ten?"

"Yes."

He nods, suddenly quiet. "There's one more. One more I should tell you, Kristi." He's holding a tortilla chip, but he puts it back on the plate and folds his fingers together. "You know it. You know what my greatest fault is."

"What? You had a zit five years ago and you haven't gotten over the shock?"

He half smiles, but it's an effort. His eyes flutter at me, and I know whatever he has to say is hard for him. "I'm a coward."

"No you're not."

"Yes. I am." He looks infinitely sad, as if he's remembering a terrible regret.

"Well, you already have ten, so we don't have to write it down. Okay?"

He seems disappointed, or frustrated, or confused. I don't know what he is. I'm tempted to listen to his thoughts to find out, but the last time I did that I found out how he saw me, and I couldn't take that again. It's too painful.

"Now you," he says as he piles a tortilla chip with a tower of beans, cheese, guacamole, and sour cream. The process seems to engulf all his concentration, and I think he must be using this activity to conquer a feeling he has inside himself. Once he has piled on more toppings than any tortilla chip should ever be asked to bear, he somehow opens his mouth wide enough to eat the whole thing in a single bite. Through the mess he says, "Your faults."

I look at him warily. I really don't want to do this, but he did it, so I can't hold back. It wouldn't be fair. Maybe if I start with the worst thing, the rest will be easier. "Well, you know those practical jokes I told you about?"

He nods.

"They're kind of mean." With a pang I remember that poor woman's bloody knee. "I'm cruel sometimes. For no reason. Other than to make myself laugh."

He writes this down without seeming to judge it and waits, his pen poised over the paper.

"I hate my mom. My dad left because of her."

He writes this down, too.

"I guess you could say I'm a misanthrope. I just don't really like people, you know? I distrust their motives."

"That's why I like dogs. They don't have motives."

"That's only three," I say with dread. It feels like slowly extracting a tooth, talking to Gusty this way. The only way I can get through this is to babble. "I purposely frustrate my teachers. I don't take school seriously. I keep a cat in the house that makes my mother sick. I have a terrible diet. I just eat pizza and chips and I drink soda and stuff ice cream down my throat at night while I watch stupid TV. I'm conceited about my intelligence, and I think everyone around me is stupid because usually they are. I don't exercise. I drink too much coffee." I remember the way the dog had been trotting down the street, a huge smile on his face. He was so happy to be free, and for the first time I wonder if Minnie Mouse is truly happy. "I keep my cat locked in my bedroom all day because I have to hide her from my mother, and it isn't fair. I never write to my dad, which is maybe why he's stayed away so long. And he's coming back on Thursday and I don't know if he means to stay or not, and I'm not sure I want him to, even though if you had asked me a week ago what I most wanted in the whole world, I'd have said it was for my dad to come back. But I don't want him anymore. I don't want him to see me. I'm fat and he'll be disappointed, and I hate him. I just hate him!"

At some point Gusty has stopped writing things down and is just looking at me, and then pretty soon the people at the next table are looking, and then the guy at the front counter is looking at me. When I realize what an ass I'm making of myself I shut up completely and hold my hand over my face, which makes me look even crazier. *What am I doing? Why did I say all that?*

I feel a hand on my shoulder, and Gusty blinks at me. His face is so sad that he almost looks ugly. He takes a napkin out of the holder on our table and hands it to me because he can see I'm nearly crying. I dab at my nose. It's totally full of snot but I don't want to expel mucus in front of him. "You're not fat," he says once I've calmed down a little.

"I'm not skinny."

"Skinny girls remind me of my sister," he says, wrinkling his nose. "Yech."

I laugh, but this makes a tear squeeze out of my eye. "I'm sorry!" I cry.

"For what?" It's not a rhetorical question. He really doesn't understand why I'm sorry, and he wants to know.

Somehow this scares me. I don't know how to answer him, and I don't know what to do. The way he looks at me is so — what? I don't like it. I don't like the way he's looking at me, as though he can see past my face into the toxic dump inside my head. I can feel his thoughts working their way through the tiny gaps in my mind. Like a trickle of water they seep through the wall I've held up between us, and I can hear them begin to drip onto my feelings, and they burn. *She's got real problems,* he thinks.

"It's getting late. I should get going," I say. "I'm sorry that I . . ." What? Had a conniption fit?

"You don't have to go, do you?"

"I'm sorry. I just — I just realized I forgot to feed my cat this morning."

"Oh, okay," he says. He seems confused. "I'll see you later?"

"Yeah." I pick up my backpack so quickly that I knock his satchel onto the floor, and everyone in the place turns to look at me again. I hold my head down and walk out of Pluribus.

I'm never going back there. I can't be with Gusty Peterson. He hurts too much.

PICKING UP DAD AT THE AIRPORT

Airports were invented by psychotic savants with an uncanny ability to pinpoint the precise level of grossness hungry travelers will tolerate in overpriced food.

We arrive forty-five minutes early only to find that Dad's flight is delayed by two hours. For the first hour we walk around and Aunt Ann buys me a pile of crap I don't need. I get a silk scarf with brown butterflies on it, a best-selling novel by some ex-marine hack, a mint green travel mug, some botanical body oil that smells like sandalwood, a Denver Broncos team jersey, a glass paperweight with a scorpion inside it, some Zuni Indian turquoise earrings, a vibrating massage thingy, and finally, because it is all getting pretty heavy, a red rolling suitcase to carry it all. Once we cover every store we get some chai green-tea decaf skim-milk lattes and two huge brownies with walnuts in them and watch CNN while we eat. Then we realize we are hungry and get personal pan pizzas and eat those, finishing it all off with fat-free frozen yogurt sundaes. I think she must have spent about two hundred dollars, and I didn't ask for a thing.

"Are you excited to see your dad?" she asks as she shovels her narrow face full of vanilla frozen yogurt dotted with tiny M&M's.

"Yes," I say, because this is the tenth time she's asked me and I've finally figured out that the only thing that will shut her up is if I tell her what she wants to hear.

"I'm excited, too! He says he's lost twenty-five pounds!" She giggles, which makes her look like a baby bird. "So have you heard from Gusty?" she asks me leadingly. She suspects there's more to the story than I've told her, and she won't let up until I break.

"No, I haven't, and I don't really want to."

"Yeah, right." She giggles. "How does he act at school?"

"I don't know. I've been avoiding him." Since my breakdown at Pluribus three days ago, I've managed not to be in the same room even once with him. Every Morning Meeting I've arrived at the last possible moment and left at the earliest opportunity. Every lunch period I've eaten with Mallory in the parking lot, and every day after school I have been the first student out the door. I just have to keep this up for the next three years and I'll never have to speak to him again.

"You need to stop avoiding the people you like, honey."

"I don't like him."

"And I don't like Russell Crowe."

"Gusty is a dumbass anyway."

"You would never have a crush on a dumbass."

"I don't have a crush on him."

She rolls her beady eyes. "I think you should give this boy a chance, Kristi. He sounds like a nice kid, and he's cute, too. That's a difficult combination to find." Aunt Ann shares my suspicion of beautiful people, though she's less draconian about it.

"He thinks I'm sick."

"How do you know?"

"Because I can *read minds,*" I tell her for the millionth time. She's the only person who knows about my ability because she's the only person I can trust with it. She only half believes me, which is fine with me. I don't have anything to prove.

"Honey, I know you're intuitive, but I don't think you're right all the time."

"I know what I know."

"Oh yeah? What am I thinking right now?"

I stare into her small brown irises. I let my mind go blank enough to receive her message and then say with a shrug, "You think I'm beautiful and any boy would be proud to go out with me, but you don't know Gusty Peterson and I do. He thinks I'm sick and psycho and that's all there is to it."

"I think you're the one who thinks you're sick, whatever that means. But I have to admit that was exactly what I was thinking. You're gorgeous, you just don't know it, and any boy *would* be proud to be with you." She winks at me, then stacks our empty bowls and tosses them into the trash can. "Let's go to the security area to wait for your dad."

I follow her very reluctantly. The pants I'm wearing are

chafing the insides of my thighs, and my shirt feels weirdly constricting. For the first time in two years I'm wearing a store-bought outfit. My found wardrobe is probably a little much for Dad to take in, and maybe I don't want to show him that part of me. So instead I'm wearing the black slacks Mom got me for Christmas and an eyelet blouse Aunt Ann picked out for me when we went to California wine country last year. She buys even more stuff for me when she's blitzed.

We park ourselves by the security gate and Aunt Ann takes my hand. One of her fingernails digs into my wrist, but I don't mind so much because she's helping me feel less shaky. I take slow breaths and practice in my mind how I'll be. I will smile slightly, but not like I'm excited. More like I'm only slightly glad to see him. I will not cry. I will not say anything to him unless he speaks to me first, and then I will give him exclusively one-word answers until we get into the car. Once in the car I will open up slightly more, just enough to give him encouragement so that he doesn't give up the idea of trying to talk to me. By the time we get to Aunt Ann's house, I will begin volunteering information, but only the kind of stuff I would say at a job interview, such as my grades, my hobbies, current interests. I will mention Mom more times than he is comfortable with, and I will say her medical career is going splendidly, which will be almost the same thing as spitting in his eye. But I'll do it innocently so he won't know I'm consciously toying with him.

That's the plan.

But when the people start filing past the security gate, my

heart rises to my mouth and all thoughts sail out of my brain. Aunt Ann is jumping up and down very slightly, biting her thin lip and kind of squealing. I stand behind her because I would rather she be the first person Dad sees when he gets here. Almost the entire plane full of people has filed past us before a balding man with blond-streaked hair, dark skin, and shining eyes comes up to us, drops his suitcase, and holds up his arms. "Hi, girls!" he cries.

It's Dad. I didn't even recognize him.

"Your hair!" Aunt Ann cries as she rushes at him. "Oh, little brother!" She starts crying.

I just stand there as they hug and hug. "Hey, little sister," the man who is my dad says. Aunt Ann is really the older sibling, but Dad calls her his little sister because she's so petite. "How you been?" he asks her, looking at me over her shoulder.

I don't like the way he's looking at me, as if he expects me to be mad and wants me to know that he's fully prepared for it. He pulls away from Ann and puts one hand on my shoulder. "Kristi. My, you've grown into a beautiful young woman."

I don't know what to say to him. I try to read his mind, but his strange face and weirdly skinny body are too distracting for me. He lost a lot of hair, but he looks a lot younger than he used to because he's so thin. The way he moves on his feet is light, as if he's ready to jump into action. He holds his head high, and his shoulders are square instead of bent like they used to be. He almost looks like a movie star. I watch him like I'd watch TV, not expecting it to watch me back.

A smile slowly creeps over his face. The wrinkles around his eyes bend, and he takes a step toward me. I can see what he means to do, so I pick up his suitcase to hold between us. "We're parked a long way from here," I say, then I turn my back on him and walk away.

DINNER AT AUNT ANN'S

Things don't go the way I planned. I thought Dad would have all kinds of questions for me, but mostly he talks to Aunt Ann. He keeps looking at me in the side mirror of Ann's Honda Civic, as if he can't believe the way I look. I let him look at me, but I don't have anything to say to him, and apparently he has no trouble containing his curiosity about me as he answers all of Aunt Ann's questions about Ebola, dysentery, typhoid, measles, tuberculosis, malaria, and parasitic worms. I can tell she's working her way up to AIDS, which gives me a little time to think strategy.

I'm not in control. I thought I would be the one fending off the questions, but Dad is too busy to ask a single one. Aunt Ann is too fascinated by disease to give him a moment's thought about anything else. I listen to him explain that Ebola is rare, even in Africa, and that he hasn't seen a case yet. And yes, there are parasites, but they aren't transmitted through human-to-human contact. That he's inoculated against most everything else and so we shouldn't worry about catching anything from him. He sounds authoritative and happy to be talking about medicine. When she starts asking about AIDS he practically jumps out of the car with excitement, talking all about how his team is heading up a national campaign for education about prophylactics. A puppeteer from San Francisco is going to give educational puppet shows to grown women about birth control, how to say no to a man, and how to look out for an abusive personality. It sounds a little patronizing to make a puppet show for grownups, but then, what do I know about African people? Maybe they like puppets. Or maybe they're just too polite to tell rich do-gooders from America when they're being condescending jerk-offs.

We finally get to Aunt Ann's tiny house, which is one suburb over from ours. It's a poorer suburb, because she doesn't make that much money as a hospital administrator, but she likes where she lives. She's surrounded by a lot of Latinos, and she shouts incoherent Spanish at them, so they love her. Near where we park the car a whole bunch of guys wearing sweaty office shirts are kicking around a soccer ball. When they see her, one of them cries, *"Mamacita, por qué no vienes para una cerveza luego, eh?"*

"No puedo, papi!" She giggles. Her face is bright red. *"Mi sobrina bellisima está en casa con mi hermano."*

They break into even faster Spanish that I can't begin to understand. I had only a year of the Language of Our Hispanic Neighbors at Journeys before the parents decided they wanted their kids to learn the Language of Our French-Canadian Neighbors instead. Aunt Ann yells something about *mañana* at them, and then we all go into her tiny house.

She has put up a banner that says, "Welcome home, little brother!" in big orange letters. She runs into the kitchen, calling over her shoulder, "Sangria all around?"

We both call, "Yes," at her, but she's already in the kitchen, leaving us alone together.

I sit down on the couch because I don't know what else to do. Dad sits in the ratty overstuffed chair across from me. He has a smile on his face just like the one he probably gives to patients before he does something painful to them. I can feel the guilt practically wafting off him. "How are you, Kristi?"

"Oh, fine," I say distantly. "How are you?"

He leans his elbows on his knees and weaves his fingers together. "I'm wondering if you're going to forgive me, I guess."

"For what?" I say very coldly. The last thing I'm going to do is make this easy for him. In fact, I'm going to make it as difficult as it can possibly be.

"For leaving, obviously."

"Oh. That."

He gets up and leans against Aunt Ann's fake fireplace, one hand stuffed into the pocket of his thin, cheap slacks. As he speaks, I get a wave of guilt and sorrow, though he's hiding it well. "You know, I really thought that you wouldn't change so much. Your Aunt Ann kept sending me pictures, but to be honest I didn't absorb it. I thought you were still that skinny little girl, that you would stay that way."

"And now I'm fat," I say, to make him feel like an asshole.

"You're not fat." He says this without looking at me. I can feel his thoughts jutting out of him, all of them tinged with shame, but the look on his face is very calm. He smiles faintly at me, and his eyes trail to the flowers on the coffee table. He seems to be hiding his true emotions, but I don't understand why he would want to hide his guilt. Doesn't he know guilt would help me forgive him? Sometimes being able to read minds makes people even more confusing. "Looking at you, I can see a lot has happened in your life since I last saw you."

Dad sits down across from me again, his eyes on the floor, and he begins to speak as if he were recounting a very distant tale that doesn't involve me at all. "You know, it was like time got compressed while I was there. I was so busy, I didn't really have time to think about anything or anyone else. That's what I needed. To get out of my own head. And so two months would pass by and it would feel like a week. And after two months I'd think, 'Well, that wasn't so long. I can stay a little longer.' And I kept staying a little longer and a little longer, until all those 'little longers' added up to two years. I looked up from the operating table one day and suddenly I was two years older, even though I felt better about myself than I ever had. But I couldn't hide the fact from myself any longer that I'd let too much time go by. That was wrong, and I won't let that happen again, Kristi."

I watch him. My face is blank, not because I'm hiding anything but because I *feel* blank, wiped out. It is strange to talk to him, to hear him talk. He's relating to me like I'm an adult, which is how he always related to me. I used to like being his confidante, but now I'm not sure how I feel about the way he talks to me. I don't understand it.

"Here we are!" Aunt Ann calls as she carries in a tray loaded with guacamole and chips, a pitcher of sangria with three glasses, and a bottle of seltzer. I feel in shock. All the questions I was expecting from Dad still haven't happened, and it makes me wonder why. Why no questions?

Dad digs into the guacamole with real gusto while Aunt Ann pours the drinks. She puts a ton of seltzer into my glass with hardly any wine, which is fine with me because I don't really like the taste of alcohol. We all sit around, Aunt Ann and I silently watching Dad while he devours the guacamole. He looks at us, embarrassed. "It's been a long time since I've eaten food like this."

"That's all right." Aunt Ann grins. "I didn't believe you when you said you lost so much weight, but I must say you look great, Ken."

"Well, it's amazing what an appetite suppressant hard work and happiness can be." He smiles at her. She gives him a nervous little twinkle, and her beady eyes dart to me. Dad doesn't notice and begins part two of his lecture about the Diseases of Western Africa and the State of Health Care in the Third World. Aunt Ann and I listen, she avidly, I quietly. He talks and talks into the night, all through our late dinner of chicken enchiladas and corn on the cob. When Aunt Ann serves us her failed experiment with homemade flan, he switches from rare tropical parasites to problems with funding for his clinic. Then, as we sip coffee in the living room, all of us melted into the furniture, Dad goes on to describe the camaraderie of the international staff in the hospital where he works. Aunt Ann finally looks at her watch and cries, "We should get Kristi home, Ken."

He yawns loudly. "Yep, it's late." We all stand. He comes up to me, rubs my shoulders, and gives me a kiss on the cheek. I let him kiss me even though I want to pull away. I have to meet him halfway, don't I? I can hear in his thoughts, *I must be careful not to push her too hard.* I guess that's nice of him. "It's a school night for you, love bug, isn't it?" he says as he sits back down on the couch.

"If you can call Journeys a school." I toss this at him like I'd offer bait to a fish.

"Oh yeah, I want to hear all about that tomorrow night over dinner, just us, okay?" he says as he puts his feet up. I let his thoughts come to me, but his mind is still eight thousand miles away. I get short flashes of what he's seeing: women wearing bright sarongs, an ancient jeep working its way around a collapsed dirt road, a sunset red with dust in the air, a field full of green tents, pouring rain. Africa.

Maybe he just hasn't come home to us all the way yet. Maybe it's too much for him to absorb, and later, maybe tomorrow, he'll really be here, really with me. "Do you mind if I don't come along, Ann?" he says as he closes his eyes. "I'm pretty bushed."

Ann nods at him, though she must know he can't see her with his eyes closed. "Come on, honey," she says softly to me. I get up and follow her out the door and into the car. We don't say anything the entire fifteen-minute drive home until we pull up in front of the house. It's completely dark, so I figure

Mom is probably hiding in her bedroom. Aunt Ann squeezes my hand and gives me an apologetic smile. "After all the excitement dies down, Kristi," she begins.

"Yeah, I know," I say, not because I agree that excitement is the reason for anything, but because I know what she's trying to do and I think it's nice of her. I can hear her thinking, *Why can't Ken see she needs a father?* She hurts for me, and this makes me feel a little less numb, which I guess is good. Maybe it's not. I don't know. I give her a kiss on her hard cheekbone and pull my new suitcase out of the back seat. "Thanks for all the stuff."

"Don't mention it, sweetheart," she says as I close the car door. She waits until I'm inside before she drives away in her buzzy little car.

Mom is either asleep or pretending to be. I've come home to a very quiet house, but the noise in my brain keeps me up all night.

GUSTY IS ZANY

By the time I get to school the next day, the pink tree is nearly bare. Petals cling very sparsely to the twisting branches, but the wind, which picked up last night, will take care of the rest. Pretty soon the nice part of fall will be over and the dark and cold will set in. I'm standing near the window before Morning Meeting begins, looking at that tree, remembering that only a few days before, I'd stood underneath it waiting for Gusty, feeling a simple happy feeling. Now that Dad has come back, I wonder if I'll ever feel a simple feeling again. Suddenly everything is complicated. It's as if the tree shed all its petals as a message to me: Be careful what you wish for.

Dad is still as magnetic as I remember him. Something about the intimate way he talks makes you want him to like you. When I was a kid, I loved his magnetism. I felt it last night, but somehow now it makes me angry. I don't want to be drawn into his magnet. I don't want to be a metal daughter again. A metal daughter is a robot. Change the batteries, oil the joints. Low maintenance.

Mom has been acting totally weird. This morning over coffee she asked me how I felt about seeing Dad again, but that was it. She wanted to hear only about my feelings. She didn't have any questions about Dad at all. I probed her thoughts as she stared into her mug, and I realized she's trying not to put me in the middle of their fight. I guess that's nice of her, but somehow it doesn't feel natural. Nothing does.

Morning Meeting is starting late today for some reason. People are milling around me, and their voices blend with their thoughts in my mind so I can listen to the background the same way I would hear the ocean. It washes over me like warm water, all those thoughts. Usually hearing what people are thinking feels like torture, but now that Dad's back, none of that seems important. It's rare when I can do this, but today I let their thoughts come and go as I watch pink petals fly away from the tree.

I feel a tap on my arm and turn to see Gusty giving me a half smile that makes his mouth look lopsided. "I've been looking for you," he says. "Are you feeling okay? You were pretty upset the other day."

The quiet feeling is suddenly gone. "I'm sorry about breaking down like that."

"Kristi, come on, we're old friends." His quiet tone makes me look at his face. He's squinting at me. I can hear that he's thinking hard about me, imagining what it would be like to be in my situation. He hurts for me. This makes me feel for a moment as if I'm not alone, as though Gusty magically climbed inside my life with me and is looking around, taking stock. "Your dad coming back, that's major," he says.

There's something so honest about him, it makes me honest, too. "Yeah, it's very major."

He rests his hand on my shoulder. "Listen, you're a tough little woman. You'll get through this."

"Hey. I'm not so little," I say, pretending to be mad.

"Yes you are," he insists with a smirk. "Allow me to demonstrate." He takes a step closer to me and rests his chin on top of my head. "You see, Kristi," he explains in a clinical tone as his voice box vibrates against my eye, "only a little woman could fit under my chin like this."

This is such a bizarre thing to do that I freeze. I expect him to step away, but he doesn't. He stands with my head tucked under his chin as if this were perfectly natural. I would be turned on standing so close to him if this weren't so weird.

"Um—" I begin, but then he swallows really hard against my head, making a very audible *glug* sound. I actually feel his Adam's apple moving against my forehead. He's totally acting like a freak on purpose, making it as weird as possible.

I decide to make it even weirder, so I continue the conversation with my mouth against his T-shirt. "So how was your night last night?"

"It was okay," he says, totally deadpan. When he talks, his chin hits my head, which makes me giggle.

"What did you do?" I say. My breath is making his T-shirt moist, which makes me giggle even more.

"Hmm, let me think." He strokes his chin, getting his fingers totally tangled in my hair, but he pretends not to notice. "Read a book about sharks. Played video games. Trimmed my toenails."

"Your toenails, huh? How'd that go?"

"Not so great. They tasted terrible."

I laugh so hard, I have to step away from him. He's laughing, too, but silently, so his face is bright red. We stand there giggling, smiling at each other for a long time, until finally it gets a little awkward and someone has to say something. "Anyway," he says, a goofy grin on his face, "the next assignment is due on Tuesday. Do you want to meet this weekend to work on it?"

"Okay. But not at Pluribus," I say, cringing.

"I'll call you Saturday morning, and we can meet up Saturday afternoon, okay?"

"Yeah."

For about ten seconds I am ridiculously happy. I watch as he trots away from me to go stand next to Eva and Hildie, who have seen the whole thing.

One eye on me, Eva tugs on his T-shirt to demand his attention. He turns to face her, and she moves in on him, wrapping one lithe arm around his neck and pulling him toward her to whisper into his ear. I want him to pull away from her—I will him to. But he doesn't pull away. I can tell he likes standing close to Eva. The way her slender body undulates as she whispers into his ear is so sexual that I have to look away.

When Gusty stood near me, it was only for a joke.

I feel shredded.

Hildie sees the look on my face and grins with satisfaction. She doesn't want Gusty getting near me. She never has, even when we were friends, ever since that day Gusty and I went behind the shed.

It was years ago, and the three of us were playing together over at their house. We made up a game with a football and a Hula-Hoop that we leaned against their dying oak tree. If one of us was able to pass the football through the hoop without knocking it over, then the other two had to do that person's bidding.

Gusty was the worst of us, which is weird since he's such a good athlete. I was the one winning. I had them get me a root beer Popsicle and watch while I ate it all myself. I made Hildie French-braid my hair even though it made her arms tired and it took forever because my hair was super long. I made Gusty walk on his hands all the way across the yard, and he could do it, too.

When Gusty threw a spiral that finally sailed through the Hula-Hoop, he stood looking at us, trying to think of what to make us do. He licked at his upper lip where a little sweat was forming, and that made me lick my upper lip, too. "What do you want us to do, Gusty?" Hildie asked as she twisted her long blond hair into a rope that bounced against her back and came untwisted again.

"Just Kristi," he said, his voice barely audible.

"Why just Kristi?" Hildie asked. She looked at me suspiciously.

"Behind the shed," he muttered, looking at the ground.

"No way," Hildie spat at him, but I was already walking around the shed. "You don't have to go," Hildie called after me.

"I have to do his bidding. It's the rules," I called over my shoulder.

"This is stupid, Gusty," she spat.

They started fighting in whispers.

I waited in the space between the wooden fence and the shed. It was dirty there, but the tree branches from the neighbor's yard leaned over the fence like a roof. Carved into the brown fence were lots of primitive figures. Most of them were four-legged animals, dogs and cats and maybe a horse or two, but one of the carvings was of two stick figures holding hands. One of the figures had very long hair, and the other was wearing a backwards baseball cap, the same way Gusty always wore his.

I heard a step behind me. Gusty was with me.

I looked at him. I was standing the way I always stood when my boobs started growing, with my right hand clasped around my left elbow. He had both hands in his jeans pockets, and his eyes kept traveling up and down my body, which was still skinny like a dancer's. I loved my body then.

"What do you want me to do?" I asked him, a little afraid of what the answer would be.

"Do you like my carvings?" he asked, and pointed.

I didn't have to look to see which carving he was pointing at. I said, "Yes. I like them."

"I did them with my knife," he said, and pulled from his pocket a large Swiss Army knife. He unfolded a couple of the blades and handed it to me. It felt heavy in my hands, sturdy, like Gusty seemed to be. I pulled the scissors attachment out and used it to cut a thread that was hanging from my dolphin T-shirt. I liked the way the blades slid back into their spots, a little reluctantly, but with a snap that told me they would stay in their place. "It's cool," I told him, and handed it back.

"My dad got it for me on a business trip. It was really expensive." He shrugged, pretending it was no big deal, so I knew it meant a lot to him.

"I like it," I said, my voice a little breathy.

He nodded at me as if he understood what I'd really meant to say even if I didn't.

"What do you want me to do?" I asked him again, surprised at my courage.

He took a half step toward me, but stopped when Hildie called, "What are you guys doing?" from the other side of the shed.

"Just *wait*, Hildie," Gusty snarled.

"Kristi! What are you doing?"

"*Nothing!*" I squealed.

"We'll be done in a minute, Hildie," Gusty told her.

She huffed, and I imagined her twisting her hair angrily.

"What do you want me to do?" I asked him again.

"Uh . . ." He seemed suddenly confused. "I don't know. I just wanted to show you my knife."

"But you have to make me do something," I said. "That's the game."

"Okay. Uh . . . c-close your eyes."

I closed my eyes, and that seemed to make my whole body wake up. I was suddenly tingly standing there, waiting for what Gusty was going to do. I wished I could stand like that for a whole hour, close to Gusty with my eyes shut, waiting for him to do something to me, but it lasted only for a second.

I felt something cold and wet in my right hand. It was slimy and soft and pliant, and I opened my eyes.

In my hand was an earthworm.

"There you go. From me to you." He smiled at me, and I knew he didn't mean it as a mean trick, but as a joke.

"Thanks. It's just beautiful," I said, and wrapped it around my middle finger like we used to do in first grade, making an earthworm ring. I held it up to him so he could see, and he smiled.

"Come on, you fags." We turned to see Hildie standing at the edge of our little green fort behind the shed. "Are you done? We're all *three* of us supposed to be playing," she added angrily.

"Stop being such a baby, Hildie," Gusty said.

Hildie's mouth dropped open and she looked at me, expecting me to say something, but for the first time I didn't take her side in an argument. I only dropped my hand so that she couldn't see the earthworm on my finger.

"What are you holding?" she asked me suspiciously.

"God, Hildie, you are so nosy!" Gusty charged at her.

The two of them erupted into an argument that made me glad I was an only child. They marched to the yard and left me alone behind the shed.

I took the earthworm from my finger and curled it into a little mound at the base of the fence, just under where Gusty had carved the stick-figure lovers. I wished I could keep my earthworm ring, but I wanted that worm to live a good long life there in Gusty Peterson's secret place.

I was too young to know what was really happening between Gusty and me. It wasn't until a whole year later that the secret parts of me started to wake up and I knocked on his door only to have it closed in my face. Somehow, though, I remember that day behind the shed as a kind of promise between us.

That's why it hurts so much to watch him standing so close to Eva. She finally releases him from her grip, but he is still standing way too close to her. He glances over at me, and I can sense in his thoughts the word *sick* fighting its way to the surface of his mind. I quickly look away.

"Hey," murmurs a voice behind me, close.

I whirl to see Mallory grinning at me. His skin looks even more flaky and grotesque, and I wince visibly.

His eyes are pained, but he forces a smile. "You've noticed. I'm doing that medication. The one my mom doesn't like? Remember?"

"You are? Is it working?"

"I don't know yet." I get a flash of him imagining himself dashing and handsome as he sweeps me off my feet and into a deeply passionate kiss.

I squint at him, trying to see beyond his acne. He might actually be kind of good-looking if it weren't for his skin. He has a long face, but it's pleasant, with sharp-looking cheekbones and a strong chin. His teeth are white and crooked in a way that actually looks kind of good. "Well, I think it's really great that you're doing it."

"Eva was the one who talked me into it." He looks across the room at her, and she gives him a huge smile before flipping her shiny black hair over her shoulder. Hildie looks to see whom Evil is waving at and narrows her slanty eyes at me. I narrow my eyes right back at her. Mallory says, "You should give Eva a chance. She's been great. We talked about my acne during one of our character education meetings, and she was really encouraging."

"I'm not surprised she'd focus on something so shallow."

"It's not shallow!" He pulls away from me as if I'd bitten him. "You try walking around like this."

I feel stung, but he's right. "I'm sorry. I didn't think about it like that."

"Anyway, Eva doesn't have it so easy. She's got some real problems, you know."

"Yeah, anorexia for one."

"So? Would that make her a bad person?"

"No, her personality makes her a bad person."

We're interrupted by the loud clanging of a bell, and everyone quiets down to look at Brian, who is twirling in the center of the room, a huge smile making him look like a deranged elf. "Attention, everyone! Are there any announcements?"

Evil Incarnate raises her hand and steps to the center of the circle. "Starting on Monday I'll be gone from school for the next three weeks, and I'm wondering if there are people in my classes who would be willing to gather my homework assignments for me? Mallory will be bringing them to me." She looks at Mallory, who gives her a thumbs-up signal. I wonder what the hell is going on between those two.

Brian calls, "Anyone who's willing to do that for Eva, please see her after Morning Meeting. Are there any other announcements?"

The spunky little freshman who always serves lunch raises her hand. Her hair is pulled tightly into the pigtails she's so devoted to. "Get ready for a special treat at lunch today! It's a chilled Russian soup that you're all going to love." She twists her mean little face into a smile, and I notice for the first time that she has a mouthful of shiny metal braces.

"She's going down," Mallory says, twisting an invisible mustache. He leans down to whisper his sinister plot into my ear.

This time there's no ambiguity. Mallory wants to stand close to me, and it's not for a joke. He can hardly keep his body away from mine.

It feels nice to know for sure that someone wants me.

MALLORY'S MAGNUM OPUS

After my last morning class I get to the Bistro as soon as I can so I don't miss anything. Mallory is already there, casing the area for the best angle of attack.

I spy the nasty little freshman standing at her usual place in line, serving the soup from a cauldron perched on a metal table. She's wearing overalls that are way too big for her. She's barely tall enough to reach her ladle into the enormous vat of soup she's doling out to people. She seems unusually chipper today, as though she is . . . proud?

I get in the lunch line behind Jacob and tap him on his now muscular shoulder. "Jacob, what's the deal with that nasty little freshman?"

"Katya?"

"Her name is Katya? So she's Russian?"

The line moves forward and I can hear her talking to a kid who has looked at the borscht with a particularly disgusted expression. "It's *supposed* to be cold!" she tells him. "You'll like it. It's my grandma's recipe."

Perfect.

I turn around and raise my eyebrows at Mallory, who has taken off his white leather jacket and placed it over the back of a chair. He has to do it soon—otherwise they'll be nearly out of the soup and it won't work. Mallory starts toward the lunch line after giving me a secret little thumbs-up.

Jacob heads for our usual table at the back of the room, but I stop him. "Let's sit right here." I point to a table near the door in case we need to run.

We sit down just as Mallory gets in line.

Jacob shouts across the table at me nonstop. "I was wondering if you could suggest to Gusty that we all go out to a movie or something, Kristi? Would you want to go to a movie with a whole bunch of people? You and me and Gusty and maybe Eva Kearns-Tate or someone like that, like a friend of Gusty's so he will feel socially secure? Hey, do you like my shirt?" He holds out a sleeve for me to look at. His shirt is a multistripe button-down that he's wearing tucked into dark blue corduroy jeans. His belt is braided leather, brown to match his loafers. He looks preppy, but in a good way.

"You look good," I have to admit.

"Thanks!" He turns to Felix Mathers, who is sitting at the next table. He has terrible blue circles under his eyes. "*Kristi* likes my outfit, Felix!" To me, Jacob says, "Felix thinks I overdid the accessories."

When he sees me noticing him, Felix turns away quickly without even acknowledging Jacob, his bony back hunched over a comic book. That guy is one weird dude.

"Jacob, why don't you sit next to me?" I pat the bench. I want him where he'll be sure to get a good view.

Jacob seems flattered and sidles near me. I get a flash of him imagining my boobs covered in pickled cabbage, and I shudder. "Gross, Jacob," I say.

"What?" he asks, then breathes into his palm to check his breath. "I brushed!"

"Shh," I say, because Mallory begins.

Mallory starts breathing hard, kind of panting, and rubs at his nose. Really loudly he makes a weird harrumphing sound. He holds his palm up to his head and lets out the first fake sneeze. "AAAACH-CHOOOO! Ahg. Excuse me!"

It was a good one. He made it sound really juicy.

I look sideways at Jacob, who says, "Oh no."

"Oh yes," I tell him.

We're both startled by an even louder fake sneeze.

This one sounds even more wet.

I had no idea how easily Mallory could command a room. The noise is so loud that everyone hushes to look at him, and that's when he lets go with the third one.

"Oh God, oh God!" he says, and does it again. "AAAAGGG-ACHOOOO!"

"Hey!" Katya screeches, her ladle poised in midair. "Keep your mucus to yourself, you degenerate!"

Mallory doubles over, panting. The people behind him in line back away. "I'm sorry!" he says. "Oh God! HERE COMES ANOTHER ONE!"

Katya leans over the huge vat of thick red soup to shield it with her body. "Stop! Sneeze the other way!" she cries.

"It's just so uncontrollable!" Mallory exclaims, and lets fly. "AAAACH! AAAACH! AAAACHOOOO!"

His body spasms, and he pretends to lose balance. His limbs flail as he dances around trying to get his feet under him. By now the entire faculty is staring at him and Brian has gotten up to help, but it's too late. Mallory trips over his own feet and, desperately trying to save himself, grasps Katya's arm. He pulls her over, and she screams, "No! NOOO!"

The entire vat of borscht topples.

Mallory saves himself, but Katya and the borscht fall headlong into the first row of tables. Suddenly the entire Bistro is awash in a tidal wave of cold, sloppy, deep red borscht, with squidlike flaps of soggy cabbage, chunks of squishy beets, and the deeply penetrating smell of garlic.

The entire room erupts into complete madness. Most people are laughing so hard, they already have tears in their eyes. The people who got hit with the first wave are standing up, picking cabbage and beets off their arms. From head to toe Katya is coated with thick, chunky soup. She is crying big-mouthed sobs as she tries to pick herself up off the floor. Brian has rushed to her side and has put one arm around her, so now his white shirt is stained with big pink blots of beet broth. I look around to see Gusty picking cabbage off Hildie's face, saying, "It's okay, It's just messy, that's all."

Mallory leans against the wall surveying the destruction. He is trying to look horror stricken and mortified, but I know him well enough to see that he is barely able to keep from laughing.

Jacob stares at the scene with his mouth hanging wide open. "Why did he *do* that?"

This question stops me. When Mallory told me what he was planning to do, I was kind of thrilled at his daring, but now that it's happening, it's a lot less funny than I thought it would be. Katya is nasty and mean, but seeing her covered in red slime makes me wonder if she really deserved *this*.

"Does Mallory hate Katya for some reason? Kristi?" Jacob grabs my elbow and shakes it to get my attention.

"No, I don't think he hates her. I think he hates . . . everything."

Why else would anyone be so cruel?

Mallory kicks into Act Two with a pretty brilliant performance, apologizing and appeasing. "Oh God! I'm so sorry! I must be allergic!" And then to prove it he sneezes again and again and again, apologizing after each sneeze.

Even if he's taken it too far, it's still kind of funny, and I find myself giggling a little. But it's not pure laughter. It's tainted with bad feelings, and I can't really enjoy it.

Once Brian has gotten Katya seated on a bench, he walks over to Mallory, squinting with suspicion. Mallory has to work a little too hard to keep a straight face. Brian isn't fooled for a second and grabs Mallory's T-shirt by the scruff, pulling him out of the room.

"Good. He's in big trouble!" Jacob says as he tastes a spoonful of his borscht. "Hey, this is pretty good!"

MALLORY'S HOUSE

Mallory doesn't come back to classes all afternoon. I peek out the window and see that he and Brian are sitting on the ground under the pink tree, which has only a few last blooms clinging to it. Brian leans against the tree trunk, one elbow on his knee, and he's listening intently. Mallory is talking animatedly, running his fingers through his hair, shaking his head. I can't tell for sure, but it seems like he might be crying. At one point Brian takes hold of Mallory's shoulder and gives him an encouraging little shake.

After school I wait on the front steps for Mallory, holding his white leather jacket that he left in the Bistro. Students file past me, including Gusty, who nudges me gently and whispers, "I'll call you," before he slaps his skateboard onto the sidewalk and speeds away. I watch him until he disappears around the corner of the school building.

Mallory and Brian finally get up off the ground, dust themselves off, and walk creakily back to the school. Mallory towers over Brian, and he keeps his head hung low. He seems to be thinking hard about something. I am absolutely dying to know what they talked about for so long.

"Hello, Kristi," Brian says to me, one eye on me and the other on the wall behind me. "I'll see you next week, Mallory," he says with a warm smile before going back into the school building.

"Are you in trouble?" I ask as I hand Mallory his jacket.

"Not like I should be," he says quietly. I read in his mind a feeling of real regret about what he did to Katya.

I was starting to have my doubts about Mallory, but this helps me like him more. He messed up, just like I did with the jogger, and now he feels as bad as I do. It's nice to have someone in my life as twisted up as I am.

We start walking toward Industrial Park. The leaves under our feet sound like crunchy corn flakes. "What's going to happen?"

"I have to make a huge pot of borscht next week for everyone, all by myself. I have to write an apology note to Katya and read it to her at Morning Meeting on Monday in front of everyone, and I can't do any more practical jokes. At all." He speaks thoughtfully, as though he's puzzled by something and grateful at the same time.

"What did Bri-bri say to you?"

Mallory holds his flaky, crusty face to the sun and breathes in as if he just woke up. "You know, he's actually a pretty cool guy."

"Cool like borscht."

"No, I mean it. He's a good person."

"What makes you think so?"

"He asked me why I thought I did destructive things some-times and wouldn't let up until I finally told him the truth." He looks at his white sneakers as they kick through the dried autumn leaves in the gutter.

My eyes trace the outline of the hill that sits right by our town. It has only a few pine trees on it. Mostly it's just dry scrub. "And what did you tell him?"

"I don't know. I just started talking. About my skin, about my dad and how he died right after I was born, about how I keep moving from school to school, about how I'm not sure my mom is such a great parent and that sometimes she seems really paranoid to me. I just talked and talked."

"And what did Brian say that was so earthshattering?"

"Nothing. He just listened."

What would I say to someone who just listened? I don't re-ally know what I'd talk about. Maybe I'd find out I'm just as frustrated about life as Mallory is.

Maybe that's why I'm so mean.

Mallory shakes his head to wake himself out of his stupor. "Want to come over?"

Dad is supposed to call me today to make dinner plans, but I'd rather get a message off the machine than talk to him. I don't even really want to see him tonight. I need some time to think. "Okay," I tell Mallory, and I follow him as he turns down a street I've never been on.

We walk to the older neighborhood in town, where the

houses are small but the yards are huge. Mallory lives in a tiny house, a lot smaller than the houses of most people who go to Journeys. It's white and kind of hunched down, so I know it's very old, and the yard is spotty and dry. Once we get through the front door, though, I see the inside is beautiful. The living room is huge, with pale hardwood floors and a stately fireplace made of some kind of stone. The mantel is a deep brown, and at first I think it's made of a wooden log cut in half, but when I get closer I realize it can't be. It's cold and hard like rock.

"Petrified wood," Mallory explains to me, and shows me the top of the mantelpiece, which has been cut off to make a smooth shelf and polished to show the ancient wood grain. "Mom got it in India."

"Cool. What was she doing there?"

"She imports stuff. She works for a furniture company as their buyer."

"Wow."

The floors are covered with beautiful red carpets woven with flowers and elephants and women carrying firewood and jugs on their heads. The couch is a shapeless mound of soft purple velvet, and I notice there is no television. Mallory sees me looking around for it and shrugs. "Mom says TV saps people's minds."

"Probably it does," I agree.

He leads me to the kitchen, which kind of reminds me of ours, only it's really small. It has nice granite countertops, white cupboards, and stainless-steel appliances. Mallory opens the refrigerator and pulls out a decanter full of an amber liquid. "Immuno-defense herbal iced tea?"

"How could I resist?"

He pours two tall glasses with ice cubes and then roots through a cupboard. "Hmm. The closest thing I have to cookies are these weird arrowroot biscuits."

"Sounds just weird enough to satisfy a girl like me," I say, wondering if his mom and mine are long-lost twins.

"Come see my room." Carrying our glasses, we walk down some stairs. Mallory's room is the entire basement, and it's even bigger than the living room. The floor is covered with white stone tile, and more exotic rugs are plopped down at odd angles on the floor. His bed is in the corner and is sloppily covered with a tapestry that pictures an old-looking building, like a mosque or a temple of some kind. The windows—really deep and wide for a basement—are covered with gauzy yellow curtains, letting in lots of light, and three beanbag chairs are arranged around a low table meant for playing backgammon. The back wall is covered with a huge bookcase so stuffed with books, it looks like it could collapse at any moment. The funkiest thing is a woven striped hammock that hangs from the ceiling.

"This is the coolest room I've ever been in."

Mallory smiles and points a remote control at the ceiling. Trippy music starts playing. "Do you like Incubus?"

"Sure."

"Come sit down," he says. For a second I'm worried that

he's headed for the bed, but instead he plops into one of the beanbags.

I take the orange one. It's hard to sit in it and keep my head up, and after a few minutes of trying I give up and just let my head rest there.

"So what's your story, Carmichael?" he asks me.

"My story," I say before taking a sip of my iced tea. It tastes like crap. "What I want to know is why Eva Kearns-Tate is missing three weeks of school."

"Sorry, top secret." I try to probe his mind to see what the big secret is, but before I can get a read on him he blind-sides me with: "Are you and Gusty going out?"

The question startles me so much that I spill on myself. "What?"

"Eva wants to know if you guys are going out, but I'm not supposed to let you know she asked."

"It's none of her business."

"I want to know, too. Are you dating him?"

It would make me sad to say no, so I avoid the question. "If he wants to date her he can."

"Okay, good," he says, and adds quickly, "Because Eva wants to go out with him."

"I don't know what's stopping her," I say, thinking of her glossy black hair and her perfectly smooth ivory skin and the way her long, lean body rested against his before Morning Meeting. Of course Gusty will go out with her—who wouldn't? She's super skinny and tall and gorgeous. Hell, *I'd* probably go out with her if I were even a little gay and she weren't such a bitch.

"As long as you're not interested in him," he says very casually, and takes a small sip of his tea. He is so carefully *not* watching me that I know watching me is precisely what he is doing. *The moment of truth* is what he's thinking.

I look at him, trying to see what's underneath his acne. In the harsh sunlight streaming through his yellow curtains, he is so red and irritated that the thought of kissing him grosses me out deeply. "How long do you have to take those pills?"

"Eight more weeks."

"That's a long time."

"But I think it's starting to work," he says hopefully, but he doesn't look at me.

"That's good."

"My mom suspects. I heard her looking through my bathroom cabinet, but I've got her beat." He pulls a small mints container from his hip pocket. "I keep them on me all day. She'll never prove a thing."

The room gets dim suddenly. A cloud must be moving over the sun outside. I look at him, trying not to be obvious about it. Now that the light isn't so bright, he looks better. The redness is diminished, and the flakes aren't as apparent. I realize that his skin is definitely less bumpy than it was. I squint my eyes and peer at him through my eyelashes. I can half imagine him as cute. I really can. But only half.

He is suddenly looking at me, all misty, and I freeze. I hear him wondering, *Does she want me to kiss her?* and I think, *Do I?*

Mallory is so much easier than Gusty. With Mallory I am in complete command of my feelings, and it feels so much safer. Shouldn't I feel safe with a boyfriend, instead of scared?

Suddenly Mallory jerks himself up to lean on his elbow, and our faces are very near each other. His lips are cracked, and there's even a little blood in the corner of his mouth, so I close my eyes.

His lips feel like cardboard as his tongue winds its way between my teeth. I feel him licking the inside of my upper lip, and then his tongue flicks along my gums and deeper into my mouth to touch my tongue. I know this is what people are supposed to do, but it feels alien to me. He kisses me for a long time and I try to like it, but mostly I just observe: his hands as they wander along my back, the way his breath feels warm against my cheek, the little purring noises he makes, as though he were a starving man and I were a filet mignon. When he pulls away from me he pants, and I can tell that he is very turned on, not just because of the wild, erotic images that are flying through his mind, but because he seems helpless. He closes his eyes as though he is in pain, but it isn't pain. He lets out a tiny groan and flops back down onto the beanbag.

"Sorry," he says, breathless.

"That's okay," I say.

This makes him pause in his panting, and he looks at me quizzically. "Why did I apologize?"

"I don't know."

"And why did you *accept* my apology?"

"I don't know that, either." I laugh nervously, and I hate how it sounds.

"Do you want to go out with me tomorrow night?"

I open my mouth to speak, but everything about me freezes. *What are you doing?* I ask myself viciously. *You don't like Mallory that way! End this now! Don't lead him on!*

Do I listen to this voice of reason? Do I look into his hopeful eyes and his acne-scarred face and say, "No, Mallory, I think we should just be friends"?

Or do I say to myself that at least he's in my league, and that he's probably getting better-looking by the second, and that I'm no match for Evil Incarnate anyway? If she wants Gusty she'll get Gusty. As if I ever had a chance with him! He's just my character education partner, nothing more. And no matter how nice and sensitive he has turned out to be, and no matter how much he acts like he likes me, every so often I catch him thinking about how sick I am. Mallory doesn't think I'm sick. He finds me sexy. And Mallory is a perfectly nice, smart guy who actually wants me. And he won't always be crusty and infected. Right?

"Sure, I'll go out with you," I tell him.

"Okay, good," he says through all the breath he's been holding. "Can I come by your house tomorrow at like six and we'll go to dinner?"

"Okay," I say. This reminds me about Dad and how we're supposed to be having dinner in like twenty minutes. But I'm sunk into this beanbag and I don't want to move. I waited for two years for Dad to come back. He can wait one more night to see me. I'll just hang out with Mallory until it's way too late for dinner, and then I'll pretend I forgot all about it. Maybe that will get Dad's attention.

Mallory presses some buttons on the remote control and we listen to a very weird song about a sophisticated woman.

It's good-enough music—it's just not my taste, really.

THE ARCADE

Because I blew off our dinner date, Dad came to the bizarre conclusion that a good way for us to reconnect would be to play hyperexpensive video games in a crowded arcade that smells of preteen-boy sweat. Their thoughts swarm at me like bees: *Don't look at that girl's boobs or it might happen again! It's always getting big like that—is that normal? Jason said that his made something the other night. Mine hasn't made anything—is that normal? I wish I could pick that booger out of my nose but that older girl is looking at me and I almost have the high score. Someday I'm going to be the best snowboarder in the country and then girls with big boobs will want me and those guys will have to find someone else to beat up.*

The inner life of the preteen boy is particularly pathetic.

Dad popped by the house this morning in Aunt Ann's little car and honked the horn until I came outside. I suppose this was his idea of a grand gesture. Mom was in the back trimming her rosebushes and pretended not to hear. My hair was still wet from my morning bath and I hadn't worked my way through my first mug of coffee, so I wasn't exactly in a great mood. He wasn't at all fazed when I glared at him. "What?" I asked.

"Let's go. I have a surprise." He winked at me the way he used to when I was twelve.

"What is it?"

"A day of raucous mad fun at the arcade!"

He barely gave me enough time to tell Mom where I'd be before he whisked me off to the mall. And now we're sitting thigh to thigh in a miniature submarine, doing combat with a cheesy-looking giant squid. Dad mans the torpedoes while I steer the vessel.

Video games were invented by demons riding dragons through the depths of a computer-generated hell rendered with excellent graphics so that I can see every drop of my blood on their three-pronged spears. I hate video games because I suck at them. When the bad guys in video games shoot at me, I actually get scared for real—I cringe and try to hide behind the control panel even though I know I am in no physical danger whatsoever. I can never hit a single target no matter how hard I try, and the stupid digital music they play grates on my opera-loving nerves. Worst of all are the thoughts bouncing around in video arcades. Violence, death, destruction, sex. Arcades bring out everyone's worst drives. Video games are agents of evil, and they should all be burned in a giant slag pit.

Dad's thoughts: *She probably never thought the old man could be so hip!*

At least I don't hear the thoughts that used to scare me so

much, about how worthless he was, about how Mom and I would be better off without him. Losing that patient really brought him low, but he seems to be much better. Maybe soon he'll start talking about moving back home.

"Fun, huh?" Dad asks just as our submarine sinks to the bottom of the Indian Ocean to be consumed by a metal-eating giant squid and its young.

"It's great." I try not to sound sarcastic, but the harder I try, the more sarcastic I sound. "Really," I add, so now I sound sarcastic and bitter. "What time is it?"

"Three-thirty."

"I'll be right back."

I go to the bathroom to check my face. I didn't even have time to put on any makeup this morning, not that I care what anyone in here thinks of me. Without eyeliner my eyes look super huge and buggy. I don't even have lip-gloss on me, so my lips look dry and cracked. My hair dried naturally, and it's all super curly and too big. I'm wearing my smiley face T-shirt and the first crinkly skirt I ever sewed, made from the set of Bambi sheets I had when I was a little girl. I look like a hippie chick from Woodstock who wandered through a time warp without her toiletry kit.

I weave my way through a group of little boys fighting over the boxing game and find the pay phone in the back of the room.

The phone rings once before Hildie picks up. "Hi," I say. "Is Gusty there?"

"Who is this?" she asks suspiciously.

"Hildie, I just need to talk to Gusty about our character education assignment."

Someone in the background asks, "Who is it?" I know that voice. Evil Incarnate is at their house. She's probably already worked her claws into his tender young flesh.

"Gusty is busy right now," Hildie tells me.

"This will only take a second, Hildie," I tell her.

"A second is a long time to waste on some people," she spits.

"Witty. Superbly executed. Now please go get Gusty."

"Okay." She laughs. I hear the phone being set down, and then a conversation ensues, loudly. "Did you know Kristi has had a crush on my brother for like *forever?*"

"No! I did not know that!" says Evil innocently.

"She actually thinks she has a chance with him. Isn't that sad?"

"It *is* sad. It's *so* sad."

"Gusty told me he thinks Kristi has *real problems.*" Hildie giggles. "She practically had a breakdown at Pluribus."

"I heard. Everyone's talking about it."

"So are you and Gusty hanging out tomorrow?"

"Yeah, he's helping me train my dog, but I know it's just an excuse to be with me," Eva purrs.

I barely hear them because my heart is thumping too loudly. I knew this would happen, but I can't help how I feel about being passed over for a beautiful person.

I drop the pay phone to let it hang by the cord and walk away aimlessly. I feel so cut down that I forget why I'm standing in a room full of little boys with painfully swollen sex organs. It even comes as a surprise when Dad taps my shoulder.

"Hey, Kristi," Dad says. "Want to play air hockey?"

I stare at him. All the emotions I'm feeling are writhing in a mass on my face.

"What's wrong?" He wraps one arm around me. "You okay?"

"Can we just go, please?" I say.

"Sure thing, honey. Sure." He guides me through the arcade. Preteen-boy thoughts ricochet around me, but they're blocked by Hildie's and Evil's mean voices in my head.

Why do I care what they think? I knew I had no chance with Gusty—it's not as if they've given me a big news flash. I still feel like I have a hatchet in my heart.

Dad leads me through the mall, past all the stores Aunt Ann wishes I would shop in, and sits me down in the food court. "Want some lunch?" he asks gently. "Corn dogs?"

I used to love corn dogs when I was a kid. That was before I discovered funnel bread. But of course Dad wouldn't know that. "Whatever."

He rushes off as though corn dogs are the key to secure familial relationships.

I sit staring at the shapes passing by me: Legs covered by corduroy, denim, twill, gingham, jersey. Feet covered by leather, nylon, Vibram, and canvas. Among them I see one familiar-looking pair of legs, semiobscured by a skateboard carried at waist level, at the bottom of which dirty, unlaced sneakers skip around, weaving through the crowd.

I know those legs as well as I know my own erotic dreams.

Of course he's here. Just when I'm at the low point in my life, as if on cue, Gusty is wandering through the mall carrying his skateboard. He works his way through the lines of people waiting to get their pictures taken and made into key chains and heads right into the arcade. He looks like he's on a mission of some kind.

My brain clicks through the chain of causality, and I know what probably happened: Gusty called my house like he said he would. Mom answered and told him I was at the arcade with Dad. Now here he is, looking for me.

I feel too confused to move. None of it makes sense. He told Hildie I have *real problems*. He thinks I'm sick and psycho. He's hanging out with Eva to help train her dog. But he keeps trying to find me, and patch things up, and get together. Maybe he just wants to get the character education assignment done, but everyone knows that it's a totally bogus project and they're not even grading us on it. He seems to want to see me, so much that he's willing to come to the mall to look for me.

"Here we are!" Dad cries just as I get up. He proudly holds out a tray with four corn dogs and two large Cokes.

"I'll be right back!" I yell, and I take off running.

I dodge through the mall, maneuvering through families with screaming babies and married people fighting with each other. I break through a group of kids all wearing identical

T-shirts and someone yells, "Hey!" but I'm already gone. I take a sharp right and suddenly I'm wrapped in the cool, crowded darkness of the arcade.

I see him at the back of the room, searching the faces for mine. I like the way he's holding his skateboard, because it makes the muscles in his arm strain against one another. His other hand is shoved into his pocket, and he's turning in a circle, squinting as he looks for me. For once he's not wearing a baseball cap, which is nice because his dark gold hair is overgrown and starting to curl around his face. When he finally turns in my direction and sees me, he breaks into a smile that frames his teeth perfectly.

He is so effortlessly gorgeous that he makes me gasp.

I smile at him. I don't even think about smiling—it's not like it's a plan or anything. I just do.

He weaves his way toward me, and I wait for him.

"Hey. You look different," he says.

I forgot I don't have on my makeup. "Um, I—"

"You look good. Natural is *good*." His eyes seem to get tangled up in my hair, which is messily cascading over my shoulder and tickling my arm.

"Thanks," I say, grateful for the darkness in here because I'm blushing so much, my ears are on fire.

"Your mom said you were here, so I thought—"

"That's good," I tell him.

And it's like we run out of words. Whatever is supposed to happen next seems unreachable. I don't know what to say, and I can tell he doesn't, either. The only thought I sense in the air is a nameless, wordless, glowy kind of feeling, but I can't tell if it's coming from him or from me. Maybe it's coming from both of us.

"My dad's in the food court," I tell him, because I'm so nervous that I can't *not* talk. "We have corn dogs," I say, and immediately cringe. *"We have corn dogs"? Did I actually just say that?*

"I love corn dogs," he says quickly.

So now the next step is to go to the corn dogs. This I can handle. Corn dogs. Okay.

Gusty doesn't make sense to me, but right now I make even less sense. I am insanely happy that he's here in the mall about to have corn dogs with me and Dad. I should be more careful, but I don't want to be careful. Even if I'm pretending that all his actions add up to something special, I want to pretend.

Dad looks surprised when we get to the table. "Oh! Hi! Aren't you"—he snaps his fingers at Gusty, trying to remember his name—"Gus? You're Hildie's brother, right?"

"Yeah, I'm Gusty." When they shake I notice that Gusty's hand is as big as Dad's.

"Have a seat," Dad says, and hands Gusty a corn dog. He gives me a quizzical look, and I dare him with my eyes to make one teasing comment. Dad gets the picture and makes like he's casual. "Nice board—is that a Tony Hawk?"

"Yeah, a Falcon." Gusty says. "You ride?"

"I used to, back in the seventies on those puny little boards with the roller-skate wheels."

"Old school!" Gusty says, and starts talking about some

documentary he saw about skate punks in California, and suddenly those two are all over the greatness of the sport and how it's unappreciated by the establishment, and I'm invisible while I nibble on my stale corn dog.

As far as I know, Dad was into Dungeons and Dragons as a teenager and basically spent his youth in darkened basements practicing magical spells and vanquishing creatures of the night. So either Dad has been keeping his love of the skate-punk scene from me all these years or he's totally faking it.

As the conversation progresses, Gusty seems to be less and less interested in what my dad has to say, and finally he casts me a quick little confused glance. I catch his thought: *Why is Kristi's dad trying to impress me?*

Before Dad embarrasses himself any further, I break in. "Dad, Gusty and I have some homework to do, so . . ."

"Oh. Okay." He seems totally crestfallen as he looks first at Gusty, his new best friend, and then me, his long-lost daughter. "I understand. That's cool. I'll give you a ride."

Dad gets quiet while the three of us walk to the parking garage, and I can feel he's mad at me. *She won't even give me a chance,* he's thinking.

Maybe you don't deserve a chance, I think back at him. But he can't hear thoughts. He's too wrapped up in his own coolness to receive the vibes of others.

It's weird—all this time he's been away, I've been super pissed at Mom, but now that he's back, I've totally forgotten about being mad at Mom and I focus all my spite right at Dad. I'm glad he feels crestfallen. I'm glad he's frustrated that the ar-

cade ploy didn't magically bring us closer together. He hasn't
even told me how long he's staying or *if* he's staying. And he
hasn't mentioned Mom or even asked how she is. So he can
take his disappointment and use it to plug up the huge leak in
his chest where his heart is supposed to be. I've got better
things to worry about than him.

He pulls up in front of the house and I open the car door,
but he puts a hand on my arm. "Gusty, mind giving us a second?" he says into the rearview mirror.

"Sure. Thanks for the corn dog," Gusty says before getting
out of the car and standing on the lawn to wait for me.

Dad blinks his eyes at me. I feel in his mind a vague fear and
I don't like it, because with Dad fear means he is about to dis-
appoint someone. "Honey, there's something I wanted to talk
to you about today."

I search his dark eyes for some clue as to what he wants me
to do with this information. I get a flash of Africa, but that's
it. "Why didn't you—"

"I was hoping that playing together would help us break
the ice and we could spend the afternoon talking. I'm guessing as I go along here."

"Guessing what?"

"How to—" His eyes drop to my chin as if he's studying a
manual on how to operate alienated teenage daughters. "I
just don't know how to talk to you anymore, you know? I'm
not sure what to say to you."

"Spit it out. Just say what you have to tell me."

"Not now. I can't now."

"Are you moving back home? Is that it?"

"No," he says as he rubs his hand over his face. "That's not it."

"So you're what? Staying in Africa forever?"

He looks up like a deer in headlights, and I read him effortlessly. He is realizing for the first time that his staying or going might actually be what *I'm* most interested in talking about. I try to read him, but all I can see are shadowy pictures of Africa and an outline of someone, someone with long hair. "I'm staying in Africa, at least for a while yet."

"Fine. Now I know. Goodbye." I get out of the car and slam the door so hard that the shocks squeak from the force. I walk toward the house, right past Gusty, who is looking at the ground as though looking at anything else is punishable by castration. I hear the buzzing of an electric window behind me and Dad calls, "Kristi!"

"What?" I reel around.

"Let's get together tomorrow, okay? I'll see if Ann will lend me her house for a couple hours. So we can talk?"

"Whatever," I tell him. We stare at each other until finally Dad looks away, starts the engine, and drives off.

Why did this have to happen in front of Gusty?

GUSTY THE COWARD

After Dad leaves, I take a couple deep breaths before I can speak to Gusty calmly. "Sorry."

He waves his hand at the ground. "Hey, don't worry about it," he says, but I hear him thinking *real problems*.

But maybe this isn't what he's thinking. Maybe I'm just remembering what Hildie said.

Somehow, when I'm with Gusty, I can't tell my thoughts from his.

I shake my head to clear it as we go into the house.

"Did you guys have fun?" Mom rushes from the kitchen, but stops when she sees Gusty with me. "Hi!" she says, surprised. She looks really disappointed as her eyes trail after the sound of Dad speeding off in Aunt Ann's car. She's wearing overalls and a tank top, and her big curly hair is pulled into a ponytail on top of her head. She's holding a spatula in one hand and a potholder in the other.

"What are you doing?" I ask her. I have rarely seen my mother interact with kitchen tools, so I'm a little destabilized.

"I thought I'd crack open one of our neglected cookbooks.

Osso buco. My mom used to make it all the time." She musters a smile at Gusty. "I'm Serena."

He smiles at her shyly. I can tell by the way he won't totally look at her that he thinks she's pretty. I need an escape now, before another parent embarrasses me. Mom is standing in front of the sliding glass door, barring our way to the backyard, so I grab Gusty's T-shirt and lead him into the garage. I try to pull him through the back door, but he stops at Dad's old workbench. "What's this?" He points at the box Dad started for me.

"It's a jewelry box," I say.

Gusty's fingers travel over the carved letters on the lid that spell my name. "It's nice. Did you make it?"

I let go of his T-shirt even though I don't want to. "My dad did. It doesn't close right."

He taps on the warped lid, cocks his head. "That would be easy enough to fix."

"Yeah, that's what my dad said four years ago." I can't help the bitter tone in my voice.

Gusty looks at me. There's so much sympathy in his eyes that I have to turn my back on him and walk out the door to the yard. He notices too much. It makes me nervous.

We sit on our big wooden furniture that we never use. Gusty looks at our lawn, which is very spotty even though Mom pays a kid from down the street to take care of it. She pays him too much, if you ask me. "You have a nice house," Gusty says.

I shrug. "It keeps the rain off my head."

His eyes wander over the rickety wooden fence behind me. "So how's it going?"

"I'm okay."

"I mean with your dad."

"Oh. I don't know."

"Is it weird to see him after two whole years?"

"*Weird* isn't the word."

"If I were you, I'd be seriously pissed at him."

"Yeah," I say. I don't really want to talk about this and Gusty understands, because he pulls a piece of folded paper out of his hip pocket.

"Ready to get down to it, Kristi Carmichael?"

"I was born ready."

He hands me the paper, and I read our assignment. *Choose one of the negative traits you listed for last week's assignment and talk with your partner about its impact on your life. Then create a plan for how you will improve this aspect of your character.* I look at him over the edge of the paper. "Is this for real?"

"You don't like it?"

"It's not their business what my problems are."

"Well, I don't think you have to tell the faculty about your problems. You just have to tell me." He pulls a pencil stub out of his hip pocket, checks the point, and then pulls out his Swiss Army knife and opens a blade.

"You still have that?" I ask him.

He lifts his eyes to mine, his eyelashes fluttering. "You remember the day I showed it to you?"

I nod.

He stares at me absently before remembering why he pulled the knife out in the first place. With a few quick strokes his pencil is razor sharp, and he folds the knife back up. "Good as new," he says. He slips the knife back into his pocket and takes the paper from me. "I'll go first because I know exactly which of my traits I want to work on."

"Which is that?"

"My worst trait. The one trait that ruins my whole life." He hesitates, but then says heavily, with great seriousness, "I'm a coward."

"No you're not. And remember last time I wouldn't write it down for you because you already had ten."

"*I* wrote it down."

"I don't see how you're a coward."

"You don't?"

"No."

"Kristi, you —" he starts, but he seems suddenly incapable of making his voice work. He takes a deep breath and forces out the words: "You of all people should know I'm a coward."

"Why me of all people? What are you talking about?"

His face turns a dark red, and he says quietly, "Never mind."

I watch as he folds in on himself. The look of mortification on his face is the same one he had that day I came to his house all those years ago when I thought he was going to kiss me. The memory sends a sharp physical pain through me, and for a second I feel angry at him. "If you want to say you're a coward, say so. It's none of my business."

"Fine, I will," he says quietly, and writes it down on the piece of paper: *Gusty is a coward.*

I watch, quietly, as he writes out a whole paragraph. With each word he sets down, his face gets redder and redder. Then suddenly he stands up, shoves the paper at me, and marches to the other end of the yard to wait while I read.

One day two years ago a girl came to my front door, and I wanted to kiss her and ask her to be my girlfriend, but I didn't. I chickened out. I haven't dated anyone since, partly because I'm too much of a coward, but mostly because I feel like I have unfinished business with this girl, and until I finish it, I can't do anything else.

I read it through twice to make sure my eyes aren't playing tricks on me, and then I look up at him.

He has turned toward me, one hand shoved into his pocket as always. He has his head down, as though looking directly at me would be painful.

First my hands start to shake, then my arms, and when I stand up and try to walk over to him, my legs shake. I take in breath to speak, but there aren't any words in my mind. I'm remembering that day when I thought he was going to kiss me and how badly I wanted it, and I'm plunged back into that time in my life when I was discovering things I had no words for.

I take a step toward Gusty, and he takes a step toward me. Then we stop. We're still across the yard from each other, but somehow there's less distance between us than ever, as if we are almost touching.

I smile at him, and he lets out a huge gush of air. I realize he has been holding his breath for a long time. This makes me laugh a little. He shakes his head, embarrassed, but he laughs at himself, too.

Any second now he's going to finish what we started two years ago on his front step. He's going to come over to me and put his arms around me, and he's going to kiss me. I know it as surely as I can see him standing there, looking at me.

Just looking.

He begins to take a step, but freezes when the doorbell rings.

When the doorbell rings, every bad feeling I've ever had in my life washes through me because I know who's at the door. Oh God, no.

I look at the sliding glass door, and I can hear Mom saying to someone, "She's in the backyard."

I see the whiteness of his outfit through the glare of the windowpane as slowly his image becomes more solid and sharp. And oh God. He's carrying flowers, and he's dressed up in a white sweater and white khakis and new white sneakers, and he's got a big smile on his face. He opens the sliding door, walks through it, closes it, and before I can open my mouth to stop him, he says, "Ready for our date?"

I turn and look at Gusty, who is staring at my feet, shaking his head barely perceptibly. Desperately I try to find his mind with my own, but all I get is an ice cube of shock.

"Gusty," I say, and Mallory turns to see him for the first time.

"Oh. Hi," Mallory says, utterly confused. He looks at the flowers he's holding.

I stare at Gusty, who rallies some kind of self-possession. "We were working on our character education assignment," he explains as he crosses the yard and snatches the paper out of my hand.

"I thought we could have spaghetti at Lou's. Or if you want, Chinese," Mallory says bravely. It is so obvious he interrupted something. It is so obvious that I forgot our date. Everything about everything is obvious to everyone.

Gusty clears his throat. "I guess we can finish your part on Monday," he says to me quietly, and brushes by Mallory on his way out. "Have fun," he tells him.

I can't even make myself say goodbye.

LOU'S

Lou's is the weirdest restaurant in our town, which is why everyone likes it. The décor revolves around one thing: the name Lou. Pictures of people named Lou cover the walls like wallpaper. Lou Reed, Lou Dobbs, Mary Lou Retton, Lou Gehrig, King Louis the Fourteenth, Emmylou Harris, Louis Gossett Junior, Lou Costello, Louis L'Amour, Lou Rawls, Louis Armstrong, and, my favorite, Luciano Pavarotti. If a customer comes up with the name of a famous Lou and his picture isn't on the wall, they get a free appetizer. But no one has ever been able to.

My favorite thing about Lou's restaurant is the fact that the owner's name is Fred. Don't bother asking why he named his restaurant Lou's. He'll just shrug and toss a basket of warm garlic bread at you. The bread is so good, you stop asking questions.

I hardly ever get to come to Lou's, but I can't enjoy it. Mallory is barely speaking and I can't even begin to think of a coherent conversation starter, so here we are, both doing impersonations of people who are utterly absorbed in the fascinating process cheese undergoes as it congeals.

"Don't you like Italian?" Mallory finally speaks, his fork halfway to his mouth. The question sounds like an accusation. I hear in the back of his mind the phrase *two-timing bitch*.

I pick up my fork, which I have just set down, and lift a lasagna noodle to look at the filling underneath it. "This is really good. I don't know what's wrong with me."

"Oh, there's nothing wrong with *you*." He stabs angrily at a meatball, and I know the charade is over. "Today you spent the afternoon with a guy who looks like he was carved by Michelangelo. There'd be something wrong with you if you *didn't* want to be with him."

"Mallory, I'm sorry—"

"But I'm hideous and you can't bear the sight of me," he says bitterly. He sets down his fork and stares angrily at a picture of Lou Ferrigno on the wall.

"You're not hideous."

"Flattery will get you everywhere," he says miserably.

"I didn't know this would happen."

"Why did you kiss me yesterday?" His eyes burn me like two hot coins.

I get a flash of him thinking about our kiss and what it had meant to him. It made him so happy. And now he's miserable, because of me.

And Gusty is miserable, too.

"Mallory, I wanted to see how it felt to kiss you. You know?"

"Because you have a fetish for infected pustules?"

"Because I like you and I wanted to see if it could work."

He shakes his head at me. I search his thoughts, but all I get is an acute ache right in the middle of his body, a terrible ache that he doesn't think he can ever soothe.

"Are you going out with him or what?"

"No."

"But he wants to, right?"

"I don't know. I think so."

"You don't know. You think so. Which is it?"

"I think he does, but we didn't really talk about it."

"Do you like hurting people?"

"Hey, I didn't know he liked me!"

"Are you trying to tell me you couldn't see he wanted you? The way he looked at you and hung around you? I saw it. Eva saw it. Hildie saw it and was totally horrified. Everyone saw it."

"I was confused." Gusty was always thinking how sick I was. How could I have known he wanted me?

"And yesterday I decided to try for you myself. I thought you could see beyond the surface in people. I thought you could see the real me under all this fucking infection!" He scratches at his red cheeks with all ten fingernails. My hand goes out to stop him from hurting himself, but he recoils. "I thought you said you'd go out with me because you wanted me instead of him."

"I didn't even know he was an option!"

"And you treat Jacob Flax like he's your little pet. If you don't like him you should let him go."

"*He* hangs around *me!*"

"Right, Kristi. You're a victim in all this," he sneers.

I feel so terrible, I can only stare at my lasagna. The cheese has become inert matter.

Mallory tosses a twenty onto the table and gets up to leave. I watch him slam through the front door of the restaurant and walk down the street toward his house.

Now that I'm alone, I remember that the restaurant is full of people. No one is talking, and everyone is pretending not to look at me. I can feel their thoughts as they zip by. *That poor boy. That girl is so selfish. How can she let him yell at her like that? Is her skirt made out of an inner tube?*

Since it's impossible to slip between the noodles of my lasagna, I do the next best thing. I quietly leave.

MOM UNMASKED

There's no way this could be chance. To have so many things go wrong in one day must mean that there is a cabal of red-eared, sharp-toothed, halitosis-ridden demons having a great deal of fun at my expense. I must be at the center of a cosmos-wide conspiracy, because when I get home after my disastrous date with Mallory, I find Minnie Mouse's litter box on the front step.

The second I see the litter box I know what happened. I was so flustered when Mallory showed up I probably didn't close my bedroom door after I got dressed and totally forgot to padlock it. Naturally this is the night that Mom decided for the first time in fifteen years to make osso buco, which probably smelled so delicious to Minnie that she jumped up on the dining table and proceeded to lick the roast with her rough pink tongue right in front of Mom. I love Minnie, but she's a total pig.

See how it all conspires together?

What I don't comprehend is Mom's bizarre reaction.

I find her sitting on the couch, still wearing her overalls and tank top. The spatula is on the glass coffee table in front of her, lying in a dribbled puddle of grease. She is holding something slender and white that glows on the end. She raises the white thing to her lips and sucks on it. She releases air from her lungs, only it's not air. The smell is unmistakable.

My health-nut doctor mother is *smoking a cigarette*.

I have to blink to make sure I'm really seeing this. My mom doesn't smoke. Smoking when you're a doctor is like playing the banjo at the Metropolitan Opera. It isn't supposed to happen.

The smoking isn't even the weirdest thing.

She takes a puff and slowly lets out the smoke before dropping her head in her hands. She hunches over, her elbows leaning on her knees, and she whimpers a little.

My mom is crying.

I have never seen my mother cry, never once in my life. We went to her grandma's funeral when I was six and she was totally dry eyed. She watched proudly as the Greek Orthodox priest sang over her grandmother's dead body, and then we went to the open casket to say goodbye. There she knelt and kissed a cross that was placed on my great-grandmother's chest. She whispered into my ear, "Do you want to kiss the cross, too, honey?" but I said no. I could only stare at the steel gray braids wound around my great-grandmother's head. Someone behind me said that she looked peaceful, but I didn't think so. She just looked very, very still.

When we got back to the pew I noticed everyone was crying except for my mom. "Why aren't you crying, Mom?"

She looked at me coolly and said, "Medical school hardens you."

That's her excuse for everything. She talks about medical school as if she's recovering from post-traumatic stress disorder. If anyone ever asks her what her surgery residency was like, she visibly shudders and changes the subject. I once asked her if she was happy when she got into Johns Hopkins, and she told me she was terrified from the moment she got her acceptance letter to the second they handed her the diploma. Mom loves being a doctor, but she hated every minute of becoming one.

She never cried about it, though. Never once. She's proud of this fact.

So to find my med-school-hardened mother crying on the couch is a bit of a shock. I consider sneaking back outside, but then the door clicks shut behind me. She hears it and leaps to her feet. She drops the cigarette *onto the carpet* and stamps it out with her toe. Then she pretends I didn't just see her do it.

"Kristi!" she says loudly, and laughs. "You're home already?"

"Yeah."

She nods spastically and begins diagnosing. "That Mallory's isotretinoin treatment looks pretty ripe. He should have his derm adjust the dosage. And you know, Gusty's growing so fast, I thought I saw a little scoliosis there. He should get checked, but it might just be his posture. Are you taking your vitamins?"

"Why are you crying, Mom? And smo—"

"Actually, I have a question for *you*." She visibly straightens.

I hear her thinking, *Who's in trouble here?* She has remembered her advantage. "Who is our furry friend?"

"Where is she?" I whisper.

"She's safe. Ann picked her up."

"Mom!"

"We're going to figure this out," she yells. "How long has she been here?"

"Just a couple months," I say, hoping the darkness in the room will mask my face. I can't lie to my mom without smirking. It's a curse.

"I see that smirk, Kristi. How long?"

"Two years."

"Hmm. Interesting." Mom starts pacing the room. "That's right around the time your dad left. Also the time I had to start working so much. Also about when my allergies began. Also when you put the padlock on your door. Interesting."

"At least I'm not a secret smoker!"

"Don't change the subject."

"I was thinking maybe I'd try smoking myself," I muse.

Mom stares at me like I've just expressed interest in heroin, but she shakes it off. "Hey! You're the one in trouble here!"

"Well, you can't exactly get on my case about dishonesty," I say, pointing to the mangled cigarette on the carpet.

From the way she looks at me, for a second I think she's *really* going to let me have it, but instead she shakes her head and goes to the bookcase. She pulls a huge book about the endocrine system from the top shelf, opens it, and from it takes a pack of cigarettes.

My mouth gapes.

She drops the book onto the coffee table and it falls open. It isn't a book at all, but a box, cleverly disguised. Inside it are all kinds of things a health nut isn't supposed to have: cigarettes, a lighter, Hostess cupcakes, and a fifth of tequila.

She crams the cigarette into the corner of her mouth and flicks her lighter at it. "I need a smoke. And anyway, there's no point in getting mad at you for living a double life if that's what I've been doing." She sucks hard at the cigarette, holds the smoke in her lungs for a second, and lets it out slowly. "Ah!" she says. She pulls her ponytail holder out and shakes her hair loose. Suddenly she looks like a slightly overweight hippie chick. She does not look like my mother.

"How long have you —"

"I started in high school," she tells me. "I quit after college. But when your dad left . . ."

I stare at her. I have no idea who this woman is. "Doctors aren't supposed to —"

"What? Be human? I smoke three cigarettes a day, five if a patient takes a dive." She holds up her hand, five fingers extended. "You'd be surprised how many doctors smoke."

I can't believe I'm hearing this. "How have I not smelled it on you?"

"When was the last time you let me give you a hug? About two years ago, right?"

I have to admit, she's right about that. I haven't let her too close for a long time.

"Honestly, Kristi." She sits back down on the couch, leans

her elbows on her knees again, and stares into space. "I didn't expect my life to be like this. You know?"

"You're chief of surgery."

"I'm a paper pusher. I miss surgery."

"Go back," I say, hoping to soften her up before we get back to the topic of Minnie's furry fate. "Give up the job. Say you made a mistake."

"Do you know how many political sutures I had to tie to get where I am?"

"Untie them."

She closes her eyes and I think she's distracted, but then I get a flash of Minnie through her mind and she straightens. "I have to think about what to do about the cat. In the meantime you can go visit her at Ann's."

"Mom, I need Minnie."

"Minnie? Like Minnie Mouse?" She smiles at me. She doesn't seem mad at all that I've been secretly waging biological warfare on her for two years. Somehow, finding Minnie made a curtain drop away. From her thoughts I can tell Mom is actually glad I've been pretending with her, because she feels guilty about pretending with me. "When you were little you always loved Minnie Mouse's fat shoes. Remember those Mary Janes she wears? You wanted a pair so bad. I looked everywhere trying to find them, but none of them looked right."

I feel a tear working loose from my left eye. What will I do without Minnie's yellow eyes beaming love at me? "Mom, I have to have Minnie. I love her too much."

"Kristi, I can't have a cat in this house. It makes me sick. You know that!"

"Then I'll live at Aunt Ann's."

Mom takes another long pull on her cigarette. "Let me do a little research, okay? There might be a solution here."

I search through her mind, and I can tell she's open to negotiations. I might get to keep Minnie somehow, but I've pushed Mom as far as she can be pushed tonight.

She leans back into the couch and the leather makes a squeak behind her. "How was your date?"

I sit in the fluffy chair opposite her and put my feet on the coffee table. I'm not supposed to do that with my shoes on, but it seems all rules are suspended for the night. "Not good. Mallory is mad."

"Because you really like Gusty, right?" She raises her eyebrows Groucho Marx–style. "He's a real hottie."

"Mom!"

"I have eyes." She crushes her cigarette out right on the glass of the coffee table. She seems sad again as she watches the last of the smoke rise from the dying ember.

"Why were you crying?"

"Oh God." She chuckles sardonically and gestures toward the kitchen. "I thought when your dad dropped you off this afternoon that maybe he'd come in to say hi. And I was going to offer him something to eat. So dumb."

This is the first time my mom has ever hinted that she wanted my dad to come back. Two years ago, when we found his note on the kitchen table, she crumpled it up and said, "Damn him." And that's how every sentence about him has ended from then on. He didn't call for Mother's Day, damn him. He didn't come back for Christmas, damn him. He didn't send me a birthday card on time, damn him. She was mad enough for the both of us, so I decided it was my job to be the one who missed him.

Now she's sad. She's really sad.

And that makes me mad. But instead of being mad at her, I'm mad at my dad.

It's kind of a relief.

"Anyway, kiddo." Mom gathers up her goody box. "You forgive me for all this?" She holds up the box like it's a visual aid.

I nod at her. "It almost makes me like you more."

"You're not going to be a smoker?"

I remember how Mallory's cigarette almost made my ribs turn inside out. "I'm not going to smoke," I tell her. My face is totally smirk-free.

"Okay. Good." She puts the box back on the top shelf. She comes over to me and kisses both my cheeks, Greek style. "I love you, you know that?"

"I love you too," I tell her. "Even though you smell like an ashtray."

We look into each other's eyes, our too-big eyes that look almost buggy. I usually never like seeing myself in Mom, but tonight I don't mind. Tonight I'm glad I came from her.

In fact, I'm proud. My mom is a bad-ass smoker. Cool.

DAD DROPS THE BOMB

When I first get to Aunt Ann's for Dad's big talk, Minnie refuses to come near me even though I'm wearing her favorite outfit—the pantsuit I made from blue silk curtains we inherited from my great-grandmother. Her yellow eyes scream, *Traitor! Traitor! Traitor!* She doesn't understand that in some situations I'm as powerless as she is.

Dad is sitting on Aunt Ann's couch under a photo of Buddhist monks creating a mandala, a circular pattern made out of brightly colored grains of sand. Aunt Ann said that after she took the picture, someone opened the door and the beautiful mandala was blown away. The monks, who had worked on it for five days, laughed.

"Ignore the cat, Kristi," Dad says, and pats the cushion next to him. "The cat will come around—just give her time."

"She hates me."

"No she doesn't. She's just confused."

He pats the cushion next to him again.

I sit on the chair farthest away from him.

Dad pulls at his collar like it's itching his neck. He gives me a brief smile, but it's wiped away from his face too quickly. Smiles that are meant to hide something never last very long, especially when the smile is hiding guilt. I can feel Dad's shame dripping off his every thought. I almost feel sorry for him.

"Do you want something to drink?" he asks me.

"No."

"I do," he says, and goes to Aunt Ann's small liquor cabinet. He pours himself a whiskey, straight up. That was the drink he had a lot when he was being sued for malpractice, when he started going downhill and thinking about how worthless he was.

I think questions at Dad, hoping that he'll want to ask them: *How is school? Who are your friends? What have your grades been like? Did you make those amazing clothes yourself? Are you dating anyone? Would you like to come see Africa? How have you managed through the past two years? Did you miss me?*

"Kristi, I have something I have to tell you. I'm not staying home for too much longer." He says all this with his back to me, as though the wall in front of him is named Kristi and he has really bad news for it.

I watch as he slowly screws the lid back onto the whiskey bottle. I remember that Aunt Ann hates whiskey but she keeps a bottle on hand for Dad. I wonder if he knows that.

"I came back home to file for divorce."

I swallow. This is not a surprise, but I feel as though the

wall named Kristi has just fallen on me. Minnie chooses this moment to jump into my lap. I'm startled, but she is head-butting my arm and purring really loudly. She still loves me — she's just mad. I scritch behind her ear, exactly in the spot she loves, and she collapses into a lump on my knees.

"I'm in love, you see," Dad murmurs.

Minnie's purring sounds deafening suddenly.

I wish I could disappear inside her fur.

Dad turns around and blinks like I'm pointing a bayonet right at his eye. "She's a brilliant internist. Her name is Rhonda Richardson. I really think you'll like her."

Dad crosses the room toward me. I notice a photo peeking out from his breast pocket. He pulls it out and hands it to me proudly. I look at it, but I don't take it from him. He is standing on a desert bluff in Africa with his arm around a thin, tall woman with a thick braid of auburn hair snaking over her shoulder. In the photo his fingers are very close to touching her right boob, but she doesn't seem to mind. Scrubby plants and rising dust surround them, and they're both smiling. They are a very handsome couple.

"She's a really amazing person. An accomplished diagnostician, but she doesn't have an overblown ego." *Like your mother does,* he might as well have said. "And she listens to me. She really listens, so I don't feel like I have to perform. I can be who I am with her, you know what I mean?"

"It must be nice to have someone who listens to you."

"Oh, Kristi, it is." He sits down across from me. "She has

been amazingly patient through all of this, and she understands that I come with baggage."

"Baggage?" I stop petting Minnie. Her claws dig into me. I let them.

He stares at me as his face reddens. "I just mean, you know—"

"Me? Mom?"

He shakes his head. "You're twisting my words."

"Am I?"

Dad closes his eyes in frustration. "Kristi, I know this is difficult. Believe me, I've agonized over this decision."

I stare at him. I do not understand this man. I could search his thoughts, but he makes me too tired. I start stroking Minnie again and her claws relax.

"I know this will have an impact on you, but Rhonda thinks that I would be doing you a disservice if I stay in an unhappy marriage. If I do, you'll only learn how to be unhappy."

"How about you leave the unhappy marriage but stay on this continent?"

"Rhonda is amazingly committed to her work there. She won't leave Africa."

"So have a long-distance relationship with her instead of with me."

He looks at me with liquid eyes. "Kristi, Rhonda has changed my life."

"What was so bad that needed changing?"

"When I met her I was very disillusioned. Twenty percent

of my surgeries were vasectomies! It had been a long time since I felt really useful as a physician."

"Feel useful as a father."

"Being a doctor is who I am!" His eyes flutter at me. He is trying hard to look at me, but he can't quite make it, so instead he goes back to Aunt Ann's liquor cabinet to refill his glass. "When I met Rhonda, I thought I'd never seen anyone so alive with purpose! She changed everything for me. I had to follow her to Africa. I had no choice." He is speaking to the wall named Kristi again. The wall named Kristi is very understanding. She accepts everything he says.

Wait. Did he just say he *followed* her to Africa?

He turns back around. "I'm marrying her, Kristi. I need her."

"You *followed* her to Africa?"

"Yes. That's right." He juts out his chin like a persecuted man who is finally claiming his identity as an American hero.

"You knew her in the States?"

"Yes."

"How long?"

"How long what?"

"How long did you know her before you left?"

Now he seems less sure of his hero status. He stares into his glass for a long time before finally admitting, "She was here doing recruitment seminars for Doctors Without Borders."

"That's not what I asked."

"She was here for two months."

I lay my hand over Minnie's small shoulders, which are as

fragile and pointy as a bird's. "You left Mom and me for a woman you knew for two months?"

He opens his mouth, but words don't seem to find their way to his tongue and he drops his chin.

"I thought you left because you were ashamed about the lawsuit!"

"Ashamed?" He shakes his head, laughs a little. "Doctors get sued all the time. That was to be expected. Besides, we settled."

"But you acted so depressed."

"I was. I knew I needed Rhonda, but I was married. I felt trapped."

"I'm a trap?"

"No, Kristi. That doesn't have anything to do with you. I felt trapped by your mother."

"How does my mother not have anything to do with me?"

"You keep twisting my words."

All this time I thought he had left because he felt worthless, like he'd let down Mom and me. But that wasn't it. He left us because some other chick made him feel like a big man.

I can't do anything but stare at his hands. I used to hold them when I crossed streets. I used to watch his hands when he would practice tying vascular sutures before a big surgery, looping quickly and easily so the patient wouldn't have time to bleed. I thought nothing could ever hurt me as long as Daddy was around to sew me up and wrap me in bandages. Back then, I never imagined he'd be the one to cut me.

Minnie hops off my lap and butts her head into the door of

Aunt Ann's bedroom, which clicks open and swallows Minnie up.

I hear a key in the front door. Aunt Ann pokes her head in with her eyes closed, calling, "It's me! Stop making out!"

She opens her eyes, and her mouth drops open. "Kristi!"

"Making out?" At first I'm totally grossed out that Aunt Ann imagined I was making out with my dad, but then I realize what it really means. I turn to Dad. "What?"

"I didn't have a chance to tell you . . ." Dad says helplessly. Seeming to accept defeat, he sets his glass down on the cabinet and calls, "Hon?"

I hear a swinging hinge, and suddenly there's another person in the room with us. She is tall and beautiful, with pink polished skin and a narrow, pointy nose. She is holding Minnie against her shoulder, and Minnie Mouse is purring like a lawn mower. "Hi, Kristi," she says with a super-warm smile.

Rhonda Richardson has been in Aunt Ann's bedroom the whole time. She has been *listening* to my conversation with my dad. She is *holding* my cat.

I turn on my Aunt Ann. "How long have you known about this?"

She backs up a half step, hugging a shopping bag to her body. "Kristi—" she starts, and looks at my dad.

"Honey." Dad reaches for my arm.

I jerk away from him and charge past Aunt Ann out the front door. They all run out to the yard, yelling at me, offering me a ride. I take off at a full run, even though I'm wearing the sandals I cut from an old tire. I don't stop running until I get to the gas station at the corner, where I use a pay phone to call Mom.

Our house is across town but she gets here in ten minutes. She honks the horn at me and I run across the oily parking lot to get in. She takes off even before I've fastened my seat belt. "What happened?" Her lips are crunched together, and I can see she's grinding her teeth.

"Did you know about this?" I shout at her. If Mom's been lying to me all this time, I think I'll lose it.

She pulls a cigarette out of her pocket and jabs it into her mouth. She doesn't light it; she just sucks on it. "Know about what?" she says warily.

"Dad has a girlfriend."

She takes a deep breath, as though she's been expecting this. "Who is she?"

"Her name's Rhonda. I hate that name."

"Tell me what you know."

I tell her the whole sickening story. When I tell her how Dad had known Rhonda for two months before he left, she finally lights the cigarette. She takes a deep drag on it and then swears through a long, steady stream of blue smoke.

"So you didn't know about it."

She's quiet for a long time and I think she's not going to answer, but she finally says, very quietly, "No."

"Dad's a selfish bastard, isn't he?"

"That's not why he didn't tell us." She pulls the car onto our street and parks in the garage before she finishes her thought: "He didn't tell us because he's"—she pauses, thinks better of badmouthing my dad to me, and substitutes a word—"afraid."

But I know what she's really thinking. She's thinking the word *coward*.

That's just what I've been thinking myself.

EXPLORATIONS OF NATURE

I come to school super late on Monday morning so that I miss Morning Meeting altogether. I can't face Mallory. And I sure can't face Gusty. I'm so depressed and strung out from lack of sleep that I didn't even have the heart to raid my found wardrobe. I borrowed a black V-neck from Mom and put on some jeans Aunt Ann bought for me a year ago. Maybe I'm dressing this way to escape detection. But really, I just don't have the energy anymore.

I get to Explorations of Nature late to find everyone has already paired off and is working noisily over their little diagrams. David is leaning over Hildie, explaining the lymphatic system of mammals to her. She straightens up as if he's the most interesting humanoid she's ever encountered and says, "So it's like phloem and xylem in plants?"

"Exactly. Excellent, Hildie." And then he reaches out with his hand and almost touches her shoulder, but catches himself and instead strokes his super-cool goatee.

I sneak up right behind him and clear my throat.

He jumps as if I'm a detective from the special-victims unit. "Kristi! You're late."

I give him a wicked grin as I reach toward Hildie's shoulder but then exaggeratedly stroke my chin, just the way he did. He blanches, and I catch a feeble thought in his mind. *Oh Jesus. She can tell.*

Poor bastard.

"We were just learning about lymph nodes, Kristi."

"Oh good! I've been thinking I should heighten my awareness of *glands,*" I say, with a meaningful glance at his crotch.

Did I mention when I get depressed I become super evil?

He clears his throat, backing away from me.

Hildie is watching me with very narrow eyes. I narrow my eyes right back at her, but I probably don't look very scary because I didn't have the energy to put on my eyeliner today.

"Hildie," David says extra briskly, to show that his relationship with her is absolutely aboveboard and completely non-lecherous. "Show Kristi today's lesson, will you?" He takes refuge at his teaching stool.

This I should have expected. Being evil always has consequences. Believe me, the universe keeps score.

Hildie stares at me coolly. Just to show her that I don't care what she and Eva said about me over the phone, I take the chair right next to her and scooch up real close. "Hiya, Hil. So you and David were talking about *nads* of some kind?"

"Lymph *nodes,* Kristi. When will you grow up?"

"How difficult. Lymph nodes! No wonder you needed extra

help from David. He's such a great teacher, isn't he, Hildie? He really *cares* about his students."

Chad Marx snickers. Hildie looks around the room nervously, and I can hear her thinking, *She can tell.* "You should keep your mouth shut, Kristi!" she whispers. "I know all about what you did to my brother on Saturday."

This hurts, but I expected her to say something about it and I have an answer ready. "Mallory and I are friends."

"That's not what Eva says."

I expected this, too. "The only time Eva should open her mouth is to eat something. She'll have to start shopping at babyGap if she loses any more weight."

"You don't know what you're talking about." Hildie shoots a desperate look at David, who has detached himself completely from her and is staring at the ceiling. "Eva is having a really hard time right now, so just shut up about that."

"I'm so glad you can be there for *someone!* The second my dad left, you stopped hanging around!"

"You were getting so paranoid! You kept asking me what I was thinking and acting so nutso! Of course I started hanging out with Eva. At least she's normal!"

"She's anorexic and evil! You call that normal?"

"You always assume the worst about people!" *You psycho bitch,* she thinks.

"I do? *I* do? You're thinking I'm a psycho bitch right now!" I shriek.

"What are you talking about?"

"Don't deny it! I heard you think it!" She's looking at me quizzically, which pisses me off so much because she *knows* I'm psychic. She was there when I was starting to figure it out, and we did all kinds of mind-reading experiments together. "You know I can read minds, Hildie. You were there when it started."

"Those were just stupid games, Kristi."

"It started out that way, but I freaked you out more than once!"

"No, that was pretend," she says, but her thoughts tell a different story. She's remembering how shocked she'd been and how she'd felt scared when I'd asked her why the words "little brat" kept bouncing around in her head. She'd turned eggshell pale and said she'd had a fight with her mom. That made me appreciate my own mother, for about a week. At least Mom has never called me a name. Not even when I deserved it.

Maybe that's why Hildie stopped being my friend. It wasn't because of Gusty or because I got depressed about Dad. Hildie stopped being my friend because I saw too much, and she was scared of me. And she still is.

"Why are you denying it, Hildie? I can hear you thinking about how psychic I am right now."

"You can hear me *think?*" Hildie stares at me, her lip curled over her perfect teeth. She feels torn. It shows on her face and in her thoughts. She's thinking about coming clean, but she's too filled with fear. She can't handle it, and so she turns on me. "Are you insane?" She laughs nervously, glancing around the room.

I suddenly remember where I am. And I notice that where I am is very, very quiet. All the other students have stopped working on their diagrams of the lymphatic system and are staring at me. I can hear their thoughts bouncing in my head: *Did she just say she can read minds? I always thought she was crazy.*

"You don't *really* think you can read minds, do you?" Hildie whispers at me, but loud enough that everyone can still hear. She's finishing me off now. Really putting on a show for everyone.

"Uh," I say. I feel like I'm having that dream where I show up at school naked and I have my whole wardrobe in my locker, but I can't remember my combination. Only this time the lock is on my mouth, because I can't think of a single word to say.

I glance at David, who is looking at me with an expression of deep concern. "Kristi." He steps forward, putting himself between Hildie and me. "Why don't you go to the Contemplation Room and wait for me there, okay?"

I could cry right here. I could lose it right this second.

I pick up my books and slink out of the room. If I had a fluffy tail like Minnie's, it would be between my legs.

I sit in the Contemplation Room and stare out the window, trying not to think about what just happened with Hildie. I imagine Hildie telling Gusty what I said, her green cat eyes flashing meanly. He'll wrinkle his face in revulsion, thanking his lucky stars he never got together with such a psychopath.

I may as well give up on him now.

The corners of the windows are misted over. It's starting to get cold outside even though it's super sunny. I wish I didn't feel so dark and cloudy in my mind.

Now everyone will think I'm crazy. They're going to send me to a mental institution. They will put me in a psych ward with people who dribble on themselves as they fight over what game shows to watch. I will go to group therapy and listen to psychotics describe their fantasies about killing their doctors. I will become extra fond of a particular brown sweater that I will wear every day. I will play solitaire and look at the birds flying outside. I will become accustomed to psychotropic drugs and cafeteria food. I will eventually become attached to the place, and I will be afraid to ever leave.

Actually, it doesn't sound half bad.

I hear footsteps behind me. David knocks his knuckles on my table to get my attention and beckons over his shoulder. He leads me to a conference room, sits down at the little table, and points at a chair across from him. I sit down, and he says, "Are you okay?"

I shake my head and shrug at the same time. I guess that means "no" and "I don't know."

"You're not looking like yourself."

"Is that such a bad thing?"

"What you said just now—"

"I don't really believe I can read minds."

"Really?" He narrows his eyes at me, and I hear him thinking, *Maybe I can get her into special ed and out of my class.*

"I was just screwing with Hildie."

"Whether you actually believe you can read minds or not, Kristi, you must recognize it's a pretty odd thing to say. Right?"

"Absolutely. That's me. Zany sense of humor."

He leans toward me, knitting his fingers together. "Just the same, I think we'll probably call your parents, okay?"

"That's really not necessary. I'm fine."

"I think it's best for me to err on the side of caution."

"What's on the other side? Indifference? Because I think you should lean toward that."

He takes my hand and holds it until I meet his eyes. "I'm not going to say anything bad about you. I just think your mom needs to know about this, okay?"

I probe him for any weak spot in his thinking, but his thoughts come at me loud and clear.

She needs help.

I hate Hildie Peterson. She keeps ruining my life.

KRISTI THE PARIAH

Only Jacob is loyal. Only Jacob is true.

He pounces on me just as I'm walking into the Bistro. "Hi, Kristi! I hear you had a weird episode in Explorations of Nature — is that right?"

"Yeah." I look around. The Bistro is especially quiet today, and everyone is looking at me. Hildie is squinting meanly as she whispers into Red Hutchins's ear. They both snigger, and then all the people around them start sniggering.

"Can you really read minds? What am I thinking right now?" Jacob closes his eyes tightly and scrunches up his nose, trying hard to send me a thought. He opens one eye. "Well?"

It is probably best not to mention the embarrassing image of my breasts coated in delicately placed bite-size mounds of mascarpone cheese, so I hazard a guess. "You are hoping I notice your new shoes. They're nice. Very retro chic."

"Wow! That's amazing!" he says, but I can't tell if he's humoring me or not.

The truth is, I'm not totally sure what he was thinking.

I get to the food line and that nasty little freshman spits at me, "Guess what I'm thinking right now."

I wait for her thoughts to ebb over me, and then I tell her, completely straight faced, "You're jealous of how big my boobs are, and you wear overalls all the time so no one can tell how flat chested you are."

That shuts her up completely. Bull's-eye.

I get a tray full of baked ziti and minestrone, which actually look appetizing for a change, but as I turn, my tray bumps Mallory and a dab of red tomato sauce lands on his white leather jacket. He gives me a look as if I did it on purpose and strides over to Hildie and sits down.

It is a strange alliance. It is a dangerous alliance.

Mallory catches me looking and glares. Head down, I run for my seat. Jacob is close on my heels.

"What am I thinking now?" He screws his eyes shut again, putting his thumbs in his ears for some reason, and bounces in his seat, waiting for me to guess.

That's when Gusty walks in the door and joins the lunch line. The nasty little freshman doesn't say a word to him when she plops ziti onto his tray, but she watches with longing as he passes by.

"Gusty," I whisper, almost without realizing it.

"That's amazing!" Jacob squeals. "How did you know that?"

"Know what?"

"Who I was thinking about. Sly thing!"

I ignore Jacob and watch as Gusty walks back toward the

table where his sister is sitting, but stops short when he sees Mallory next to her.

"Gusty!" Jacob yells. "Come sit with us!"

"Jacob! Don't!" I try to stop him, but he is already waving Gusty over with his long, skinny hand.

"You bad girl, reading my mind—you've known all this time!" he hisses at me.

"Known what?"

"About my feelings!"

"Jacob, we're just friends, okay?"

"You and Gusty? I know! Because he's gay, right?"

This totally blind-sides me. I stare at him. "Why would you think Gusty is gay?"

"Tell me he is! *Please!*" Jacob whispers just before I feel Gusty's presence next to my right shoulder. "Hi, Gusty!" Jacob calls. "We have room here if you want to sit with us." Jacob flashes him a milky white smile. I don't mean milky because his teeth are white. I mean milky because he's drinking milk.

"Hi," Gusty says. He makes himself smile at me. He really tries.

"Hi," I whisper at him.

He sits down next to me, casting me little side-glances. He picks up his fork and stabs at a limp ziti.

"Gusty, I'm—" I start.

"Don't apologize." He searches my face, the corners of his lips turned down.

My heart feels suddenly weak, and I can feel my face melting as I look at him. He's staring into his baked ziti with those green eyes of his. He feels so far away. I reach out to him with my mind to try to read him, but all I can get is a heavy feeling of regret.

"Gusty," Jacob busts in, "I was interested in learning how to skateboard. Do you think you could teach me about it? I don't have very good balance, but I think I could learn if I tried really hard. I wouldn't want to do it on stairs or anything. Not right away. But ramps would be okay. And sidewalks, of course."

"Sure, Jacob. If you want me to," Gusty says before standing up with his tray.

"Okay, great!" Jacob says to Gusty, positively glowing.

"Let's talk later, okay?" Gusty says to me. His eyes flutter at me, but he can't look at me.

"Okay," I say. I lean my head into his line of vision, but he only smiles vaguely in my direction before he walks away.

I watch as Gusty sits down with his skate buddies. He opens his milk carton very slowly, as though he's too sad to do anything quickly. Everyone else at his table is talking and laughing, but he's on the other side of the planet.

This can't be the end. If he's this sad, he must still want me. I just need to explain everything. I need to figure out how.

I turn back to my food and start picking at the pasta. I can't eat, though, and I put down my fork. "Want my lunch?" I ask Jacob.

He doesn't hear me. He is smiling across the room at Gusty Peterson as though he's trying out for the Olympic Smiling Team. He sees me looking at him and blushes like crazy. He twists happily in his seat as he stabs a ziti with his fork and nibbles on the end of it. "I guess I have a little crush." He's so happy, he's spitting again. "What do people wear skateboarding? I mean, I want to look good, but I don't want to try too hard."

"What are you talking about?" I ask as I wipe his spit off my shoulder.

"My date! With Gusty!"

"Jacob, two guys hanging out is not a date."

He tilts his head, offended. "I never expected this attitude from you, of all people."

"What attitude?"

"What Gusty and I do behind closed doors is our business."

I stare at him with my mouth open while it all clicks into place.

Jacob Flax is gay?

How can he be gay? I've caught him imagining my breasts in a million different ways. It can't be. "You don't mean that you want Gusty?"

"Come on, Kristi. To see Gusty is to want Gusty."

It takes me a minute to process all this, and while I do, I stare at Jacob. He's wearing a crisply ironed blue shirt, perfectly fitted jeans, and a black leather belt that matches his lace-up oxfords perfectly. His book bag is made of canvas with leather trim that also matches his belt, and for the first time I notice he's wearing a musky cologne. As he eats he takes small bites and chews them thoroughly, dabbing at the corners of his mouth with his napkin, which he keeps on his lap.

Jacob Flax is totally gay.

"Jacob, Gusty is straight. Believe me. I know for sure."

"Haven't you ever noticed he never has a girlfriend? I'll admit he's pretty masculine, but no one with hair like that could be straight."

"His hair is naturally curly."

"No way, Kristi. There's got to be some gel involved, at least. And a diffuser attachment on his blow dryer. Probably an ionic one."

"Jacob, Gusty is not gay."

He stares at me as his lips droop farther and farther toward the floor. "Then why would he teach me to skateboard?"

"Because he's a nice guy?"

"But he must have known I was hinting for a date!" Jacob says. He is seriously dismayed.

"Oh, Jacob, how could you think he's gay?"

"I don't know. I hoped!" He picks up his napkin to hide his face.

Jacob Flax is trying not to cry.

"Jacob, pull it together!"

He sniffles, looking at me with completely bewildered, tearful eyes.

"If you weren't so far in the closet, maybe Gusty would have known you were asking him out!"

"What the hell are you talking about?" He throws down his napkin and levels a glare at me. "The whole school knows I'm gay, Kristi."

"No they don't."

"Uh, yeah, they do."

"Jacob, *I* didn't know you were gay!"

He stares for a minute before he finally finds his voice. "You? *You* didn't know? You're like my best friend!"

"Well, if *I* didn't know, how can you be sure everyone else knows?"

He is completely taken aback. "You are really self-involved, Kristi, you know that?"

"So the whole school knows you're gay, is that it?"

"Yes, Kristi. The whole school knows I'm gay."

"So prove it." I fold my arms over my chest and stare at him meanly.

He stares back at me just as meanly. "Fine, I will," he says. Suddenly he stands up on his chair and claps his hands over his head. "Excuse me! Excuse me! Everyone! Could I have a moment of your time please?"

Slowly the noise of competing conversations trickles to a murmur, and people turn to look. Hildie has a cranberry juice halfway to her mouth. Mallory has turned to watch Jacob, but when I catch his eye, he looks away.

"Is there anyone in this school who does not know that I'm gay?" Jacob booms over everyone's head, and I realize that his voice has begun to change. Yelling at everyone like this gives him a certain . . . dignity. "Please stand up if you didn't know I'm gay. Anyone?"

People start glancing around the Bistro. Gusty turns to look, too.

"Seriously, everyone knows I'm gay, right?"

I see Mallory shrug, and reluctantly he stands up. "I'm new," he explains. This gives a couple other people courage. A freshman who wears plaid every day stands up, along with a girl who compulsively draws hearts on her notebooks. But that's it.

Jacob turns to me, one eyebrow arched. "Kristi? Shouldn't you be standing?"

I can't stand. I don't have the energy to stand.

I don't understand this. If Jacob is gay, why the hell is he always picturing my boobs?

Why didn't I know my mom is a secret smoker?

Why did I think Dad left because of the lawsuit?

Why do I always hear Gusty thinking I'm sick?

If I'm so damn psychic, why couldn't I see the truth, that Gusty is in love with me, Jacob is gay, and my mom is a semi-cool cigarette smoker, and my dad . . .

My dad is a cheating bastard.

KRISTI THE NUT-JOB

When I come home from school, a weird van is parked outside our house and Mom is smoking a cigarette on the front steps. She's wearing blue jeans rolled up above her ankles and an old Rolling Stones T-shirt with a huge tongue on it. When she sees me she beams like a halogen bulb. "Hey, honey."

"Hey, what's this?' I point at the van, which has big yellow letters on the side: HEAVEN SCENT CLEANING SERVICE.

"Having the carpets and upholstery cleaned to clear out the cat dander. Also, I have a surprise for you."

She waves me over, and I follow her around the house. I try to search her thoughts, but then I remember that I might not be psychic and so I stop, but not before I hear her voice in my mind saying, *I hope she likes this.* When we get to her scraggly rosebushes, she stops and watches my face in anticipation. I don't see what I'm supposed to be looking at, except maybe that the grass is getting leggy. "What?"

She proudly points at my bedroom window. "See?"

A strange hinged contraption is wedged under my window sash. "What is that?"

"It's a kitty door."

"A what?"

"Now your cat can come and go as he pleases!" She watches my face, all hopeful. "Do you like it?"

"She."

"She, then."

I can tell Mom wants me to be thrilled, but all I can think about is my sweet little Minnie Mouse getting eaten by a pack of pit bulls. "Minnie's not an outdoor cat."

Her smile deflates. "She's not?"

"No, she's never been outside since I got her."

"So she stays cooped up in your room all day long?"

"Yeah," I say, feeling guilty about it.

"Well, honey, this is the best compromise I could come up with." She pulls at the little strands of hair at the nape of her neck and starts twisting them, which is what she always does when she's starting to lose patience. "You can let her into your room, but nowhere else in the house, and she can rule the yard."

"I don't think it's safe."

"Not as safe as being inside all the time, but it will sure be a lot more fun for her, wouldn't you say?"

"But she doesn't have survival skills."

"You could've fooled me! It took me an hour to get her into the laundry hamper the other night. She's a vicious little minx." She throws her cigarette onto the lawn and tamps it out with her toe. "Look, it's the best I can do. This is the only way she can live here."

"Can't she just stay in my bedroom full-time?"

"I'd rather she spend at least part of the time outside, hon. It'll cut down on the dander. And it's more fair to her."

I'm about to launch a protest, but the phone rings like a bell signaling the end of round one and she jogs around the house to answer it.

I go over to the weathered furniture on our lawn. We've neglected it too long, so now stripes of mold are growing up the legs of the chairs and table, making patterns on the wood grain. I kind of like how it looks. I also like the tiny spiders that hide in the table. I've learned over the years to sit with my legs out to the side so they won't crawl on me. Though it wouldn't matter if they did. They're just babies.

Maybe it isn't such a bad thing if I'm not psychic. I always thought I was kind of special, but I never felt good being psychic. I just felt freakish and hurt most of the time. What worries me, though, is this: What the hell are all those voices inside my head? Am I nuts?

Mom comes back, walking slowly across the lawn. There are two deep worry lines between her eyebrows. She glances at me with her dark eyes, trying to read me, and I realize what that phone call was probably about.

"So you can read minds, huh?" Mom sits down across from me very slowly, as though a sudden motion might make me dangerously psychotic. "Your science teacher says he's concerned."

"David's an idiot, Mom. You shouldn't listen to him."

"I didn't speak to David. Brian's the one who called."

This bums me out. Does the entire faculty know what happened now? "Great. What did Principal Bri-bri have to say?"

"He said David was concerned about your mental health, but he apologized for that. He said, 'Not everyone is open to the paranormal.' I thought that was weird."

Somehow I'm not surprised Brian would be open to my psychic abilities. He seems like the type.

Mom's eyes study me. "What's going on here?"

"Nothing. A little argument with Hildie is getting blown way out of proportion." I shift my eyes onto Mom's reflection in the sliding glass door. It makes her look whispery and vague, but I can tell from her posture she's not happy.

"Should I be worried here?"

"No." I laugh, but I know I seem nervous and fidgety. The truth is, maybe Mom should be worried. I'm a little worried myself.

"Kristi, do you really believe you can read minds?"

I look into her eyes. She's giving me her best doctor deadpan, but I can still tell she's worried that I'm crazy. "I'm not sure I'm psychic, but my invisible friend is."

She smirks. "Big pink bunny?"

"Oh, you've met?"

Mom chuckles, shaking her head. "Gammy would love this."

"Who?"

"Your great-grandmother. She claimed she could hear thoughts," Mom says. "Honestly, I always thought she was a little nuts. But I loved her."

I remember that day she and I stood over my great-grand-mother's casket, the way my mother kissed her cross and how she didn't cry.

"You know the last thing she said to me? She told me never to smoke. It was emphysema that killed her. At the age of ninety-three." She laughs as she takes out a cigarette. She holds it up to the sky and says something in Greek before lighting it.

"What does that mean?"

"It's a Greek saying. Uh—*The fox is one hundred years old, the child one hundred and ten.*" She smiles, and I notice how smiling makes her pretty. "Whatever that means. She used to say it about you."

"What else did she say?"

"She told me to watch after you because you were special." Mom shakes her head. "I let her down on both counts."

I look at Mom a long time. She is staring at the blades of grass at her feet, her thoughts very far away, though I can catch just the tip of them. She's thinking: *I thought I'd be a better mother.* But maybe I didn't hear her thoughts. Maybe it's just an intuition, like Aunt Ann says. "Mom, you know"—I wait until her large olive eyes fix on mine—"I didn't want you to watch me."

"I know." She nods. But I can see it doesn't help her feel any better. "So, Kristi, are you a nut-job or not?" She's only half joking.

I think about it. Really think. It's not as though I hear voices telling me to jump off bridges. Thoughts sometimes occur to me, and sometimes I believe those thoughts belong to other people. So what if I sometimes get it wrong? Maybe that makes me less psychic than I thought I was, or maybe not psychic at all, but does that make me nuts? "No, Mom. I'm not a nut-job. I'm confused maybe, but I'm not crazy."

"Okay." She nods again, and I can see she believes me. "This is a confusing time for both of us, honey. It's okay to be confused."

It's nice to know that Mom can trust that I'm okay, even if the rest of the world thinks I'm crazy.

I look around at our faded lawn furniture and the high wooden fence. There are certainly plenty of places for Minnie to hide. I imagine her weaving through the blades of grass, stalking a defenseless bird. Maybe it wouldn't be so bad to let her out every so often. She might like it.

REVELATIONS

The next day my body attends class, but my mind keeps turning everything over. I thought I always knew what people were thinking. Now I can't be sure. As I walk through the halls I catch snippets of thoughts—*She's so psycho. Why does she look so sad? He'll never forgive her.*—but I no longer know if the thoughts are mine or someone else's. How am I supposed to go through life like that, not knowing what people are thinking?

I felt so safe when I was sure of my powers. I had everyone figured out, and that way they couldn't hurt me. But really I didn't have anything figured out. And I still got hurt anyway. I got hurt a lot. By Hildie, Gusty, Dad. And I hurt other people, too. Mom, and Jacob. And Mallory especially.

Is it okay to let other people be a mystery to me? Should I believe my eyes more and my head less?

I wish I could know for sure. Am I psychic? Do I want to be?

Thinking about this makes my palms sweat, and I have to stop before I make myself crazy. Slowly I start concentrating on my classes, and slowly the jumble of everyone's thoughts fades into white noise.

I run into Brian just as I'm coming out of the Bistro after lunch. He pounces on me and, hooking a talon over my shoulder, says, "Let's talk."

"I have class in ten minutes."

"I'll okay it with your teacher," he says, and pulls me down the hallway without giving me time for another excuse.

He leads me outside, across the lawn, and we sit under the same tree where he'd talked to Mallory. He leans his fat back against the skinny trunk, and I can hear the little tree groan under his weight. I sit across from him, Indian-style, and press the ends of my fingers together to await his words of wisdom.

"I thought we should talk a little about what happened yesterday in Explorations of Nature."

"I think that whole thing has gotten blown out of proportion, Brian."

"You're probably right, but we should still talk about it." He takes a deep breath. He seems unsure about something, as if he's trying to figure out what he can tell me and what he should keep private. Finally he launches into it, his voice low and frank, addressing me as an equal—very different from the Brian of Morning Meeting. "When I was seventeen years old, I had a terrible nightmare that my childhood buddy was trapped in a cave under the ocean. He kept calling my name from under the waves and I tried to dive down to save him, but I couldn't fight the current." He squints at me, pausing long enough to let me guess how his story ends. "The next morning we learned he'd been killed in a flash flood."

"That's awful," I say. Stories like this freak me out. I've never had a premonition about death, and I don't want to.

"If you talk to people, most of us have had experiences like that. Some more than others." He waits for me to volunteer something, but I keep quiet, so he goes on. "How long have you suspected you were psychic?" he asks.

His manner is so straightforward, it sort of brings out my honest streak. "I guess it hit a couple years ago."

"What was your first experience?"

I'm quiet for a second because I'm not sure I want to talk to him about this, but something in the way he's quietly waiting helps me feel it's okay to talk. "A couple weeks before my dad left, I knew he was going to leave us."

"And you're the only one who knew?"

I nod.

"That's a heavy burden."

"But I'm starting to wonder if maybe I'm not as psychic as I thought."

He shrugs, his eyes wandering over the clouds above us. "We all have to live with a measure of uncertainty in our lives," he says. He leans his head back against the tree. "What would it mean if you weren't psychic?"

"I'll have to go through life guessing."

"Guessing what?"

"Whether I can trust people."

"That's true for everyone, Kristi." He smiles at me very

warmly, which makes me nervous, so I focus on the ground in front of me. A little red beetle is crawling up a blade of grass, which bends under its weight, so the beetle just ends up back where it started, on the ground. Brian says: "Trust isn't a black and white thing, you know. Everyone has the capacity to let you down at one time or another."

"Then why should I trust anyone?"

"Because if you can't trust, you can't love." His good eye is on me, and he's giving me this look as if he's really trying to *reach* me. It's so annoying.

"Gee, Brian, if you put that to music maybe Barry Manilow will record it."

He surprises me by laughing deep from his belly. He laughs so hard, I can't help giggling a little with him. Just a little, though.

During Story as Cultural Artifact I sit in the Contemplation Room, where I'm supposed to be working on an essay about the relationship between Dostoyevsky's *Crime and Punishment* and Nietzsche's theory of the Superman, but I can't concentrate. I hear the whisper of an opening door, and Gusty walks in with a notebook under his arm. When he sees me he pauses for just a second, but then seems to make a decision and walks up to my table. He smiles a hello.

"Hi," I mouth.

He sits down across from me. My blood is pounding through the veins in my ears and I'm shaking. I have so much to say to him, but I don't know how to start.

He scribbles something onto his notebook and holds it up for me to read. *Let's take a walk.*

I nod, and we both get up and walk quickly out the door. I don't know if our teachers saw us or not. I don't care.

Gusty leads me out to the front steps of the school and gives me a long look before sitting down. I sit next to him. We're both quiet for a while, but I know it's really my job to begin. "I'm sorry about what happened on Saturday, Gusty."

"You don't have to apologize."

"Just the same, I'm sorry."

He nods, but he still seems troubled by something. I can tell he doesn't really want to bring it up but feels he has to. "I talked to Hildie. About your fight yesterday. A lot of people heard you say some pretty weird things, Kristi."

I feel suddenly cornered. I expected him to ask about Mallory, not about this. "So? You've never said weird things?"

He breathes out hard. "Is it true? Did you say you could read Hildie's mind?"

"So what if I did?"

"Don't you know how strange that sounds?"

His face is carefully blank, but I can see the fear in his eyes. I hate how he's looking at me. It makes me feel so . . . *sick.*

I want to prove to Gusty I'm not crazy so that he'll never look at me like this again. I probably shouldn't do this because I might not be psychic, but talking to Brian gave me more confidence. Besides, if I have a connection with anyone, it would be with Gusty, right? "Close your eyes," I tell him.

"Why?"

"Close your eyes and think of an image. Think about it hard."

He seems taken off-guard, and I can tell he doesn't want to do it, but then I put my hand over his eyes and he closes them.

I tune out the sound of the trees sighing in the wind and try to focus only on Gusty.

At first it feels as if I'm spinning, and I have to take deep breaths. Then I get an image, but what I see makes me feel shy. I wait to make sure it's real, but then I realize there's no way to know for sure anyway, so I just blurt it out. "You're thinking about the carvings behind the shed in your backyard. The ones you showed me that time." I crack an eye open and look at him. He's looking at me, but I can't read his expression. "Did I get it right?"

His eyebrows crunch together. "I was thinking about that dog we met."

"Oh." I feel crestfallen, but I try to laugh it off. "So much for my psychic powers."

Gusty nods slowly, like he's expecting me to start spouting prophecies about the end of the world. "So you really believe you can read minds?"

I could lie to him and say no, it was all a big joke. But I don't want to. I want him to know the real me. "For a while it seemed like I was unusually . . . intuitive. Now I'm not so sure. Do you think I'm crazy now?"

"I don't know *what* to think." He shakes his head, bewildered.

This should make me feel hurt, but it doesn't. Instead, I'm

boiling-oil mad. I've had about enough of Gusty Peterson's uncertainty. "Look, Gusty. Either like me for who I am or don't. I don't care anymore, okay?" He bites his bottom lip like he's trying to find the right thing to say, but I don't want to wait around for Gusty anymore. I want to hurt him. "Chicken out a second time. Be my guest."

I stand up and start to pull open the school door, but I feel a hand on my arm. I turn around to see a seriously pissed-off Gusty Peterson. "You know, maybe I chickened out with you, Kristi, but you haven't exactly been easy to approach!"

"So your being a coward is *my* fault?"

I shouldn't have said that. I shouldn't have called him a coward. His face flushes, and a tremor seems to move through him. When he opens his mouth I expect him to yell, but instead his voice goes very deep and very quiet. "*I'm* the coward? You're completely closed off, Kristi. You sit in an ivory tower, and you pass judgment on everyone else. Because you're the one who's afraid."

We stare at each other in silence.

I'm so hurt, I can hardly speak above a whisper. "Well then, I guess you're glad we never got together."

"I didn't say that." He reaches toward me, and before I can pull away he's buried his hands in my hair and pulled my face toward his. Very softly he says, "I *forgive* your faults."

Part of me wants to give in to the plaintive way he's looking at me, but I hate what he said too much. Who is Gusty to forgive me for being who I am? "I didn't ask for your forgiveness. And I don't care what you think of me."

I pull away from him and walk back into the school building. Part of me wants to cry, but I won't let myself. Instead I calmly walk back into the Contemplation Room, find my table, pull out my chair, and sit back down.

I am perfectly calm. I do not care about what just happened. It doesn't affect me at all.

I'm well into the second page of my essay before it hits me like a punch to the stomach. I told Gusty the truth about reading minds because I wanted him to know the real me. But he does know the real me. I'm judgmental, and I never let anyone too close because I'm afraid.

Every word he said about me is true.

MALLORY

I feel like the scum that grows at the bottom of a dirty shower curtain. I feel like the sponge that mops up the scum and then is left wet on the rim of the bathtub to continue growing the scum. I feel like the starving rat who finds the scum on the sponge and has to make the decision: eat the scum or die?

I feel awful.

I keep going over my fight with Gusty, and I can't figure out what it means. He said he forgives my faults, but do I forgive him? Because even if what he said is true, it was still really crappy to lay me open like that.

Is Gusty the jerk, or am I? Are we both jerks?

How many things have to go wrong between us before we finally just accept the fact that we're not supposed to be together?

At the end of the day I'm putting my books away in my cubbyhole when I see Mallory weaving through the crowd. He's carrying two backpacks, one draped over each shoulder, and he seems to be in a hurry. I position myself near the front door so that he has to walk past me. He glances through me for half a second before breezing right by.

Now I feel like the poop of the rat who has eaten the scum off the sponge.

Without even thinking about why, I follow him, brushing past people milling in the hallway. I try to clear my mind completely as I walk out the doors into the dim autumn air.

Mallory is walking fast, and I slink along behind him. He cuts across the park behind Journeys, past the bench where we waited for a victim for our practical joke. I pause for just a moment to touch the graying wood with my fingertips as I pass by. Then I quicken my pace behind Mallory.

It's windy, and the sky is full of clouds. The leaves sound like crinkling paper when I step on them, and I can smell that beautiful scent of autumn. It's the smell of decay, but somehow it smells so green and true.

With the leaves twirling around him and his wild orange hair standing up, Mallory looks like a white wizard striding through the park. I have to jog to keep up.

He turns onto Miller Street, kicking up dust behind him. I'm starting to get a stitch in my side, but I keep following.

I don't know why I'm doing this. I am too afraid to talk to him, but I want to see where he's going. Somehow I think if I can follow him, I might see some sign that he will forgive me and I can feel a little less sad. But that's stupid. Life doesn't work like that. You don't really get signs. But sometimes hoping for a sign is all I can do.

Mallory walks a long way down Miller Street, past the little houses that all look alike, with slanted carports and gravel on the roofs. After he crosses Colchester Avenue, he walks by the big houses where the doctors live. Each house is grand in a false way. One is made entirely of stone, another has thick wooden beams, and another looks like the kind of monstrosity Scarlett O'Hara would live in. Finally Mallory turns in to the hospital parking lot and walks toward the front door.

I know what he's doing. He's going to see Eva.

I hang back behind a fake ficus tree and watch while he talks to a receptionist with penciled-on eyebrows. She points to the hallway on the left, and Mallory takes off again. I follow behind him, careful not to be seen. He winds through the tiled hallways at a fast clip. He finally stops before a ward that's closed off with two heavy double doors. I hide just around the corner near a cart full of gross-smelling food and listen to his conversation with the receptionist.

"I'm here to leave some things for Eva Kearns-Tate."

"Your name?"

"Mallory St. Croix."

"I need to see if you're on the list. One moment." I hear the clicking of computer keys, and then she says, "Okay. You need to empty your pockets. I'll give you everything back when you leave."

"She's not in here for drugs."

"I still need you to empty your pockets, and I'll need to look through those bags."

I hear a couple zippers and then lots of shuffling, as if the nurse is sifting through Mallory's backpacks.

What kind of unit is this?

Once she approves the backpacks, she gives him something to wear on his wrist and then I hear a loud buzzer go off. Soon I hear the voice of a man say, "Follow me," then the thunk of the heavy doors closing behind them.

Finally I can peek at the sign on the doors. All it says is INPATIENT WARD.

What the hell does that mean? Is that for chronically ill people? Does Eva have some kind of horrible disease?

I know there's one person here I can ask—the chief of surgery. I follow the hallways back to where I came from, looking for the surgery ward.

I haven't come to my mom's workplace for a few years, but it's still familiar. They have lots of arrows painted on the walls to help patients find their way from one department to another. There are fake plants everywhere that my mom wishes they would take away. It seems as though there's always someone mopping the floor and there's always something beeping and buzzing. When I finally find Mom's new office, I stop to read the nameplate. It says SERENA THEOPHILUS, M.D., CHIEF OF SURGERY in large white letters. The door to her office is open and I poke my head in.

She is sitting behind a pile of charts two feet thick. She rubs her forehead as she scribbles. In the middle of a sentence she seems to get an idea and mumbles into a little tape recorder. She seems tired and stressed out, but she also seems really competent and smart. For the first time in a long time, I'm proud of my mom for who she is and what she does. She cuts into people to save their lives. She is the chief of surgery in a big hospital. That's pretty cool.

I wait quietly, watching, until she closes one chart and picks up another. Then I clear my throat.

"Kristi!" She stands quickly, almost knocking over a big pile of papers. "What are you doing here?" She seems crazy happy to see me.

I shrug as I take a chair across from her. It's fake leather and makes a farting sound as I sit down. "I just wanted to check out your new office."

She spreads her arms wide to show off how big the room is. There's a large philodendron drooping over a tall file cabinet. On the wall behind her is a tapestry of a human face composed of different geometric shapes, all in brown. It's very ugly, but it's interesting to look at, too. There's a frame propped on her desk next to her phone. I don't have to look at the picture to know it's a photo of her, me, and Dad that we took for a Christmas card five years ago. I hate how I look in that photo. My face is too round and my eyes are too big, and I'm smiling like a red-faced maniac. I complained about that picture, but Mom loved it because she said everyone in our family looked really happy. It makes me sad that she still keeps a picture of Dad around.

"It's nice in here," I tell her.

"It sure beats having nothing but a locker." She leans back in her chair, studying me. Strands are pulled haphazardly from the bun in her hair. "You know, honey, that phone call from Brian got me thinking. Maybe it's time to pull you out of Journeys after all. Give you a chance for a fresh start."

I can't believe my ears. "Where is this coming from?"

"Well, you've been complaining about the school from day one. And it struck me as very strange that Brian apologized for a staff member assuming you *can't* read minds. That seems a little kooky to me." She raises her eyebrows. "How about it? Want out?"

Now's my chance to escape Journeys forever, if I want to. I'd never have to go back to Explorations of Nature to learn about how Robert Frost informs the study of cellular biology. I'd never have to sit in the stupid Contemplation Room scratching at homework. I'd never have to listen to Brian exuding his joy in life during Morning Meeting. I've been wanting an escape from Journeys for a long time, but suddenly I don't want to leave. It's weird, it's crazy, it's loopy, but where else would the principal entertain the possibility that a student has psychic powers? It's probably the only school in America where I halfway fit in. "I think I'd rather stay," I tell Mom.

"Wait!" Mom picks up her tape recorder and points it at me. "Can I get that on tape?" I think she's kidding, but she pushes record.

To humor her I say very clearly, "I, Kristi Carmichael, still think that Journeys is totally bogus, but I don't want to leave."

"*Totally* bogus?" she asks testily.

"Well, fifty percent bogus."

"Okay, then." She clicks her recorder off, smiling. She

seems proud of me. If I didn't know better, I'd say I can feel it coming out of her. I even get a quick flash of myself through her eyes. For a second I hear her thinking how grown up I look and how pretty, but then I remember I'm probably not psychic after all. Old habits. One thing I do know for sure, though: my mom kind of admires me. At least, she's looking at me like she does.

I guess I kind of admire her, too.

But I'm not one to dwell on mushy crap like this. I'm here for a purpose. "I was walking around earlier," I begin, carefully choosing my words. "What's the inpatient ward for?"

"It's for the mentally ill, mostly. But they have a drug-treatment program there and a clinic for eating disorders."

"Like anorexia?"

"Yes, like that." She narrows her eyes at me, suddenly suspicious. She can sense an ulterior motive lurking behind my wide, innocent eyes. "Why do you ask?"

"Why do people need a clinic just to start eating again?" I ask. Blink, blink, innocence, innocence.

"Anorexia isn't that simple, Kristi. Don't you know that?" Her eyes trail me up and down, checking to see if I'm starving myself, which is a real laugh.

"Don't worry about me, Mom. I'm not so caught up in my looks that I'd stop *eating* just to get skinny."

Mom grinds her teeth the way she always does when she's offended. "Kristi, people don't become anorexic out of *vanity*."

"Then why else?"

"I don't know. Control? Fear? I'm not a psychiatrist, but I've seen enough organ failure in anorexics to know it kills plenty of people. And it's an awful way to die." She shakes her head, seeming to relive some distant memory of a patient.

This makes me think. All this time I've made fun of Evil Incarnate for being anorexic. I never thought that she might *die* from it.

If she weren't evil, I would apologize to her. But she'll just have to settle for a cease-fire.

"So," Mom begins, weaving her fingers under her chin. "Dad's coming over tonight."

My stomach drops and I have to catch my breath. "Why?"

"He owes us that much, don't you think?"

"He owes us more," I tell her, but I swallow hard. After everything that's happened, I don't want to see him.

"You don't have to be there if you don't want to. Ann and you could go to the movies."

This is tempting, but slinking away seems a pretty cowardly thing to do. I should be there. This is my family, and it's important. "No. I'll come home."

She nods, and I can see she's even prouder of me.

Mom and I agree to meet at home at six o'clock, and I head toward the front of the hospital to start my long walk home. I'm following the yellow arrows, deep in thought, so I don't even see him before I turn the corner and ram right into him. "Mallory!"

"Oh. Hi," he mumbles. His hand goes up to the red patch on his neck. The skin still looks a little raw, but I can see there's no more infection. Now that his skin is better, I can notice his nose is straight and narrow, and his lips are full and even. Mallory is going to be a good-looking guy soon, and for a moment I wish again that I could want him. But even knowing how handsome he'll probably be, I still don't want him the way I want Gusty. I can't imagine wanting anyone else that way. "What are you doing here?" he asks, his eyes hooded and wary.

"My mom works here," I say, glad I don't have to admit I followed him.

"Oh." He tucks his hand into the pocket of his white jeans and waits for me to say something.

There's only one thing to say. "Mallory, I'm sorry," I tell him. "I didn't mean to hurt you."

His eyes skirt over me, unsure. He bites the corner of his lip. "What happened to your clothes?"

I look down at the blue T-shirt and jeans I'm wearing. "I didn't have the energy."

"Well, you shouldn't dress just like everyone else. It's not you."

"I know." We stand there dumbly, each of us looking over the other's shoulder. Part of me wants to run away, but I know if I do we'll never be right again. It's now or never. "Mallory, Gusty and I have unfinished business. It's been that way since long before I met you."

"Eva told me." He nods abstractly.

"She's really sick, isn't she?"

"In a way you and I can't imagine." His brown eyes light on the floor.

I look at him while I try to get my courage up. He seems worried and burdened, but he no longer seems angry at me. He shifts his weight as though he wants to leave, so I finally make myself say it. "Our friendship means a lot to me."

He blinks at me. He makes no move to speak.

"Mallory, I just hope you can forgive me someday."

It seems to take a lot of effort, but he forces the corners of his mouth to turn upward. "I hope so, too," he says before he walks away.

I can only watch him go.

SHALLOW

Mom and I sit on either end of the sofa, waiting. It's seven-thirty and Dad still hasn't shown up. Mom glances at her watch and shakes her head angrily. "If that bastard—" she starts, but stops when she hears an engine outside. We hear the slam of one car door, and then another. We both stand to face the door, waiting for Dad to come in, but the doorbell rings instead. Mom pauses, as if she's surprised, like I am, that Dad wouldn't just walk in the way he used to. "Come in," she calls. As the door swings open, I pray under my breath that Dad doesn't have Rhonda with him.

He doesn't. Aunt Ann is standing next to him holding a pet carrier. She's brought Minnie Mouse home. She smiles sheepishly at me as I take the carrier away from her. I look inside at Minnie, who seems thoroughly freaked out, and take her back to my bedroom. Aunt Ann follows me, whispering, "Your mom looks good. How's she taking all this?"

"I don't know," I say coldly.

I go into my bedroom and think about closing the door on Aunt Ann's face, but that's too cruel even for me. She kicks her way through the dirty laundry on my floor. I kneel on the carpet to let Minnie out of her carrier. Quietly Aunt Ann closes the door behind us. I keep my back to her as I carefully pull Minnie out and hold her to me. I can feel the vibration of her purring against my throat, and I bury my face in her fur. She smells faintly of Aunt Ann's lemongrass perfume.

Aunt Ann plops down onto my bed and waits until I look at her. "Kristi, I know you're mad at me, and I don't blame you."

"Why would I be mad at you?" I say into Minnie's fur.

"Don't be coy." Her fuzzy hair is hanging wispy in her eyes. She tucks a strand behind her ear, gathering courage. "I didn't tell you about Rhonda because I thought your father should be the one."

"How long have you known about her?"

"A while." Her eyes drop to the floor. "I kept thinking it wouldn't last between them and that he'd come back and you'd never have to find out. I was trying to protect you."

"You were trying to protect him."

"I was trying to protect you both."

"I feel like I'm at the center of a conspiracy," I spit at her. Minnie pulls away and strides toward the closet to look for her litter box. I watch her go because I no longer want to look at Aunt Ann.

"Maybe I should have told you, Kristi. I didn't know what to do." She leans back on my mattress. The covers are bunched up underneath the small of her back. It can't be very comfortable, but she doesn't seem to notice.

She's quiet a long time. I catch myself trying to read her

thoughts, but all I get is a deep, long wave of terrible disappointment. Besides, I'm probably not psychic. I have to stop doing that.

Finally she takes a breath. "You know, I've idolized your father for a long time. He was all the things I could never be. Brilliant. Good-looking. Confident." She laughs. "He was four years younger than me, but I was the one following him around, wanting to hang out with him and his friends. Isn't that pathetic?" She glances down at me, but I don't give her anything. My face is carefully neutral. "It's a sad thing when your hero turns out to be—" She considers the words, but I can feel her back away from them. She's trying to protect me again.

"It's not your fault, Aunt Ann," I finally say. "Dad's just the way he is, and there's nothing we can do about it."

"I know." She half smiles and looks toward the door. We both pause to listen to the murmur of Mom's and Dad's voices. It's an ancient sound from my childhood, and as it washes over me I'm flooded with grief and longing for the days before Dad left, when I was innocent and things were simple. As I feel the first tears fall, I lean my head onto my knees. Aunt Ann's hand rests on my shoulder, and she sits with me in the darkness, waiting for Mom and Dad to finish their talk.

It's a long time before we hear a knock on the door. Dad pokes his head into the room and says in a flimsy, cheerful voice, "It's dark in here!" He turns on the light and smiles down at us.

Aunt Ann pops up and simply walks out the door, holding her purse to her side. As she passes by Dad she gives him a cool stare, but he pretends not to notice and smiles at me again. "So, I see your housekeeping skills remain the same." He gestures toward the laundry strewn all over the floor.

"What did you and Mom talk about?"

He sits on the bed and slaps his hands on his knees. "How would you like to come to Africa for a visit?" He shoots a diluted smile in my direction. He's trying to act cheerful and confident, but I sense a deep rift inside of him. He knows that what he's doing is terribly selfish and he doesn't want to face that. "Rhonda and I fly out on Saturday. We'd like you to come see us, maybe even for Christmas break?"

"I'll think about it," I tell him, but at the moment a cozy Christmas, just the three of us, sounds about as much fun as dysentery. "You're leaving Saturday?"

"I have to get back." He blinks sadly at me.

Something in me shuts down, and I turn away from him to look at Minnie. She is lying in her old spot in my half-open sock drawer, crinkling her yellow eyes at me, purring. I look at her, begging for help because I don't know how to have this conversation. I want to make Dad understand how badly he has hurt me, but I know that's impossible because Dad is too shallow to understand a deep hurt.

I look at the wrinkles around his eyes. His skin is tanned, but the center of each wrinkle is white. I guess the sun never reaches the creases in his skin. "Do you remember that jewelry box?" I ask him.

He stares at me, totally blank.

"The one you made for me?"

He gasps. "Oh yes! I'd completely forgotten about that!" He glances over the top of my dresser, looking for it. "Do you use it?"

"You never finished it. It doesn't close right."

His lips part as he remembers, and suddenly he stands up. "I can fix that. Where is it?" He is filled with sudden purpose, as if fixing my jewelry box would definitively prove his worth as a father and a human being.

"It's in the garage." I barely finish the sentence before he's off, racing toward the garage, every step filled with take-charge authority. Dad is here! He's going to fix his little girl's jewelry box if it takes him all night!

I follow him down the hallway, past Mom and Aunt Ann, who are sitting at the kitchen table, a bottle of tequila between them. They're both bleary and watch us curiously as we trudge out to the garage. I turn on the light and point at Dad's workbench. "It's right where you left it," I tell him.

"Where?" I follow his blank stare.

It's gone.

Dad and I look at the rectangle left in the dust where the jewelry box had sat for so long. "What happened to it?" Dad asks me.

I know exactly what happened. I feel sick, and I have to sit down on the step behind me. "Someone must have taken it." I swallow hard. Why would Gusty do this?

Dad sits down next to me and wraps his arm around my

shoulder. He looks just like his old confident self, but now that he's touching me, I can feel that deep down he knows how much he's let me down. "I'll make you another one, Kristi," he whispers. But he knows how empty this is, how little it helps.

I can't stop the tears from falling. Dad wraps his other arm around me and buries his face in my ponytail. We sit together like that long enough for his tears to soak all the way through my hair.

After Dad and Aunt Ann leave, I find Mom sitting in the backyard working her way through the bottle of tequila and a pack of cigarettes. For the first time since I've known her, she seems very small, like she needs protection.

Looking at her like this, I think I know what it was about Mom that Dad didn't like. She doesn't seem to need anyone. She's strong, and I resented her because a lot of the time, even if I wouldn't admit it, I felt very weak compared to her. But looking at her now, shaky and wasted, I know that she needed my dad a lot, and now he's run away with some other woman.

She still has me, though.

"Mom. You okay?"

She turns her head toward me and smiles with one side of her face. "No. How are you?"

"Ready for a shot of tequila and a smoke." I'm kidding, but she actually pushes the bottle toward me, though she puts her hand over the cigarettes.

I take a small swig and immediately want to spit it out. "Jesus. It's like jet fuel!"

"That's why the Indians called it firewater." She chuckles. The breeze picks up, swirling her wild hair around her head. She looks like a Greek goddess.

"Mom, I'm sorry about Dad."

"Don't *you* be sorry. Let him be sorry."

"He really is a jerk for cheating on you, isn't he?"

She takes in a deep breath. "Oh, I don't know. He changed. He wanted something else. Someone else. What I can't forgive is the way he left you."

"I'll be okay."

"I know you will be. You're your mother's daughter." She slides her eyes over to me and grins.

I watch her face in the moonlight. Her skin looks delicate and frail. There are lines around her mouth and circles under her eyes. For a second I pretend I'm looking into my future, seeing myself at her age, and I decide that would be okay. I wouldn't mind ending up like my mom.

Except I'd want a smaller ass.

I remember what Gusty said, about how I judge other people, and I realize that I did this most of all to Mom.

"Hey, old lady."

"Hmm."

"I'm sorry I hid Minnie from you," I say, kind of as a primer, because the rest of what I want to say is really going to hurt coming out. "And I'm sorry I've been such a bitch for the past two years."

She looks at me quizzically and laughs. "Can I get that on tape?"

"No. Sorry. You had one shot at it. That's it."

She turns away, a relaxed smile on her mouth. I made her happy for a change, and that makes me feel nice and warm inside. Or maybe it's the tequila.

GUSTY

We're all standing in a big circle waiting for Brian to start Processing. It's Friday, the end of the worst week of my life, and I can hardly wait to go home. Brian swings his bell and it clangs through the noise of the crowd. Slowly the room trickles into silence. "Well, we've had quite a week! Does anyone have any announcements?" He turns in a slow circle, waiting for someone to speak up. When his eyes meet mine, he pauses and raises his eyebrows.

I've never made any kind of announcement before, but almost without thinking about it, I step into the center of the circle and clear my throat. Brian is giving me a chance to redeem myself. I may as well take it, but I'm not going to say what he expects me to. "There are some people here I've hurt. And I want to say I'm sorry. I didn't mean to hurt you. It's hard to be left behind, and I've been left behind by a lot of people who were important to me." I look at Hildie, whose face has turned bright red. "I just want to say I'm going to try to be nicer. But in the meantime, there's one person here who has something of mine, and I'd like it back."

At this, Gusty lifts his face and looks at me. There's a long yarn of sadness stretched between us. I wish I could pull it toward me to bring Gusty closer, but making the announcement took everything out of me, so I simply walk back to join the circle around Brian. A few other people make announcements, but I don't listen to them. Finally, everyone joins hands like we do every Friday afternoon, and we sing our school song. The lyrics are based on a poem by John Keats, and for the first time I really hear the words:

> *The journey homeward to habitual self!*
> *A mad-pursuing of the fog-born elf,*
> *Whose flitting lantern, through rude nettle-briar,*
> *Cheats us into a swamp, into a fire . . .*

After Processing is over I look for Gusty, but I feel a tap on my shoulder and turn to see Jacob Flax standing next to me. "Hey, Kristi." He still seems mad at me, but not as mad as before.

"Hi, Jacob."

The corners of his mouth are turned down. He looks like a textbook definition of the word *forlorn*. Suddenly I'm overcome with an impulse, and I wrap my arms around him and hold on tight. He is stiff at first and I can sense he's a little stunned, but after a second he wraps his arms around me, too. Now that I'm close to him, I can tell he's wearing cologne. "You smell good," I tell him.

"Thanks," he says, but he steps away from me quickly.

"I haven't been a very good friend, have I?"

His eyes widen. "Are you kidding? You've been great!"

"Really?"

"You're like the only person who's always been honest with me!"

I look into his eyes to make sure he isn't just saying this to make me feel better, but he seems perfectly sincere. "You know what, Jacob? You're pretty much my best friend." I am surprised to hear myself say this, but I find it's really true.

He smiles, but there's sadness in the way he ducks his head. "So are you and Gusty an item or something?"

"Maybe," I say gently. "I hope so."

He wraps his arms around his middle. "I guess I have to work on my detection skills."

"You're not the only one." I walk out the front door into the cool autumn air, and Jacob follows. Now that I know he's gay, I feel so much more relaxed around him. I'm even comfortable enough to say: "For some reason I actually used to think that you thought about my boobs a lot. Can you believe that?"

Jacob stops stock-still. His face turns chalky. His pale eyes fasten on me, and his mouth pops open in astonishment.

"What? Don't tell me that you actually *did* picture my boobs!"

"No! Of course not! I'm gay!" Suddenly he's running down the school steps so fast, it's a wonder he doesn't generate a sonic boom.

"Hey!" I grab hold of his arm and force him to slow down. "Why are you running away?"

"I'm not!"

"Jacob, did you used to picture my naked boobies?" I can't hide my smirk.

"No!" Now he's breathing so hard that droplets of spit escape from between his lips.

"Obviously you are lying, Jacob."

He tries to assume a deadpan expression, but he can't do it, so finally he gives up. "You don't understand, Kristi! It's Felix Mathers's fault!"

"Felix? That weird dude?"

"When we walked to school together, anytime he saw you he'd say something disgusting to me about your boobs. He's obsessed!" Jacob looks so revolted that any second he might actually physically crawl out of his skin.

"Calm down, Jacob. I believe you."

"He said so much stuff about you that it got into my head! Any time I saw you I'd remember his sick fantasies. It drove me crazy!"

"It's okay, Jacob."

"You better stay away from Felix Mathers, Kristi. He is a very troubled boy."

"I will, Jacob."

He's so freaked out that it actually makes him look kind of manly, because he's staring hard and he's breathing in a really aggressive way. "Why do you have to be so psychic?!" he demands of me.

I shake my head, bewildered. "I was starting to think I wasn't!"

"Really?"

"Well, yeah. I mean, come on. Reading minds? It's kind of kid stuff, isn't it?"

He sees the sense in this, and nods agreement. "Maybe you were responding to physical cues or something."

That must be it. I was extrapolating from his body language. "Like how you used to stare at my boobies all the time?" I say with an evil grin.

His face twists. "Gross, Kristi."

"You did! But anyway, Jacob, it's not my business what you were thinking."

"That's right!" I wait while Jacob pulls himself together. He rearranges his scarf and pats down his hair. "That was very upsetting."

"It's all over now, Jacob." And it really is. It's even kind of a relief to be more normal than I thought I was.

It's chilly outside. I snuggle into the coat I made from an old Hudson Bay blanket, glad it still fits. Even though I miss the pink cotton-candy tree, I don't mind the changing season. Autumn is such a comfortable time of year, when drinking hot chocolate and reading books and huddling up with Minnie is all there is to do. And I love doing all those things.

"There's this guy at the gym I kind of like," Jacob tells me as we continue down the school steps. "He looks at me a lot, too. I'm not sure if he's in high school, or maybe he goes to college. Maybe I'll get the courage up to talk to him."

"Is he cute?" I bounce down the stairs beside him.

"He's totally hot. He's Hispanic, or Mexican. Anyway, I think I like the tall, dark, and handsome type even more than

I like the Viking type." He pauses, his gaze fixed on something in the distance. I turn to look.

Gusty is leaning against a narrow tree trunk, watching us. He seems to be waiting for me.

Jacob smiles. "I'll see you later. Call me." He walks down the sidewalk, hugging his canvas barn coat around himself against the sudden wind.

Slowly I close the distance between Gusty and me.

He tries to smooth his overgrown curls out of his eyes, but they pop right back to where they had been before.

"Hey," I tell him.

"Hi." He gives me a sad smile, his eyes on the red stripe of my coat, following it all the way to the ground.

He starts walking, so I start walking, too. We go slowly. He kicks into the tiny pebbles that have collected in the gutter, and some of them spray my brown lace-up boots.

"I'm sorry," he whispers.

"It's okay," I whisper back.

"I mean about what I said," he whispers again.

"I know."

He is quiet walking next to me, and he doesn't seem to know exactly where we're going. The way he walks, with short kicking motions, makes me think that he has his eyes closed. But when I look at his eyes I see that they're wide open.

"So did you decide I'm not crazy after all?"

"I never thought you were crazy. Just a little . . . confused." This hurts, and I'm about to really let him have it, but he holds up his hand to stop me. "I mean about Mallory and me."

"Oh. I only said I'd go out with Mallory because I didn't know you liked me. I didn't think someone like you could ever like someone like me."

He lets out a little puff of air. "What is that supposed to mean?"

"Come on, Gusty. You know what I mean." He goes back to kicking at the small rocks in the gutter. "You could have any girl you want. Any *guy*, for that matter."

He laughs.

"Eva Kearns-Tate *likes* you, for God's sake. She's never been my favorite person, but I have to admit she's gorgeous."

He nods again. "Sure. She's very pretty."

"So? Why would I think you'd want me when you could have her?"

"Well, geez, I traded character education partners so that I could work with you."

"What?!" If it's possible to be thrilled and shocked at the same time, that's what I am. "You traded partners to work with me?"

"I had to pay Farid Amir twenty dollars so he'd work with that weird girl who's always drawing hearts on her notebook."

"I had no idea!"

He stares at me like I'm a very slow child. "You never even *looked* at the bulletin board, did you?"

I shrug, and he rolls his gorgeous eyes. Now I'm embarrassed and happy at the same time. Gusty sure knows how to mix up my emotions.

He seems to feel mixed up too. I want to make him happy

if I can, so I say, "Gusty, if I'd known you liked me, I wouldn't have gone out with Mallory."

He's quiet for a while, so I don't know if my explanation worked, but finally he says, "I guess there's no way you could have known I liked you. It's not like I really told you."

"I *should* have known. Mallory said he knew. He said everyone knew, except me. And Jacob Flax, I guess."

He grimaces. "Yeah, that announcement at lunch got me thinking—maybe he likes me?" He looks at me tentatively.

"Nah, he likes a guy at his gym," I say nonchalantly, figuring Jacob will probably want to save face. I'm a bitch, but I can be a nice bitch. Sometimes.

"Kristi." Gusty takes a deep breath and forces himself to face me. He grabs both my shoulders and looks into my eyes with such intensity that I know this is costing him effort, as though he's mastering something inside of himself. "I like you better than Eva because I like your spirit. She's a nice girl, but I like how fiery and dangerous you are. You're smart, and you don't let anyone walk on you. And when your dad left, you were so brave about it, even though I could tell it hurt you. After Hildie blew you off I thought you'd get depressed, but instead you came to school wearing the coolest clothes I'd ever seen, and you acted like you didn't even care that your best friend totally abandoned you."

"I did care," I whisper.

"But you didn't give her the satisfaction of knowing it. That took guts."

"So I'm the fat girl with the great personality?"

"No! You're curvy and soft." He seems to have stopped thinking about what he wants to say. He's just saying it. "I love the color of your skin, and your thick hair — I just want to mess it up. And your huge eyes. You have the biggest, most beautiful eyes I've ever seen, and I love the way they change color, from being almost black indoors, and then they become this deep olive green when the sun hits your face. I love the way your lips look like candy. I love the way you smell. I don't know if it's your shampoo or your perfume. Maybe it's just pheromones. I don't know, but I love it. I've never smelled it anywhere else. Kristi, I really like you. Will you go to the Halloween dance with me?"

Now that it's my turn to speak I can't, so I nod.

"Okay, cool," he says. Suddenly looking directly at me seems to be too much for him, and he starts walking again. "Will you sew your own costume?"

"I kind of *have* to sew my own clothes. Most shirts don't even fit around my ginormous — " The words catch in my throat, and I look at him.

He's smiling, a little crookedly, and his green eyes are glowing at me. "Your ginormous . . ." He whirls around, and suddenly our chests are touching and I can feel his breath on my face. He raises an eyebrow. "Your ginormous personality?"

I shake my head, totally embarrassed.

"Kristi, you have a totally *sick* body. You should *not* be ashamed of it."

I stare at his face in open amazement. "*What* did you just say?"

He suddenly gets super embarrassed and mumbles, "I think your body is . . . nice."

"You said *sick!*"

"Yeah." His eyes dart around, a little perplexed. "It's a skater word. If someone mungs a primo grind . . . you know? It's sick."

I'm speechless. I can only stare at him, my mouth open, my eyes sending out rays of happiness. "So, in skaterspeak, *sick* is *good?*"

"Yeah! *Sick* is awesome."

Gusty is smiling at me like he's almost ready to laugh, and that makes me want to crack a joke. "So *sick* is good . . . I have much to learn. Will you teach me the ways of your people?"

"Oh, lady, I'll get you your own board, if you want."

"Okay, if you'll listen to my *Carmen* CD with me," I say. I have a feeling that's a good opera to start him on.

His eyes smile into mine, but then he opens his backpack and starts fishing through it. "I have something for you," he says.

I know what it is, and I'm so relieved. "Why did you take it?"

"You'll see." He pulls it out. It's wrapped in a piece of black velvet tied with a ribbon, which is a beautiful deep purple. I untie it and shove it into my pocket to save so I can wear it in my hair. The velvet slides off the box, and I gasp.

He has fixed it. It closes with a perfect seal that looks airtight. "You fixed my box for me?"

He nods. "I rubbed it with a beeswax finish to preserve it.

The grain is really pretty now, isn't it?" I run my fingers over the butter yellow wood. It feels velvety and smooth, almost like skin. I open the box and see that he has lined it with the same black velvet he wrapped it in. It's the most beautiful thing I've ever seen.

"I love it," I whisper. I'm so moved that I could cry, but I don't want him to see, so I put my arms around him and lean my face onto his shoulder. He can probably feel my tears on his neck, but I realize I don't care if he knows I'm crying. I don't mind at all.

We hold each other, and I can feel the vibes moving between us. It's more than the flashes I get from most people because I feel his thoughts through my whole body. Every message and whisper coming from his mind is deeply warm, like sunlight through stained glass.

I pull away to look at him, at his lips. His tongue flicks along the bottom edge of his teeth. I'm looking at his mouth because I can't bear to look into his eyes. If I do, I know something in me will break and flood all through me. I'll be lost, swimming, trying to breathe, trying too hard, if I look into his eyes.

But I can't help myself. I look.

And he's looking at me. Just looking.

I can breathe. I'm drowning, but I can still breathe.

He takes a deep breath, pulls me toward him, and he kisses me.

Autumn leaves are swirling around us, and Gusty Peterson is kissing me.

We move together as if we're dancing, and I love letting him lead. For the first time in my life I let go completely, and I melt into him.

After everything, it's possible I really did hear Gusty thinking I was sick—I just didn't understand what he meant! Maybe I *have* been receiving psychic vibes; it's just that my filter was on the wrong setting.

Or maybe it was clogged with all my negative crap.

I guess life is a big guessing game, no matter how much I think I know.

But I don't have to guess about this: kissing was invented by silken-haired angels with violin voices and dewdrop eyes.

And I'm still me, a big-breasted, slightly freaky, opera-loving, possibly psychic seamstress and cat enthusiast who now has a totally hot boyfriend.

ACKNOWLEDGMENTS

Thanks to the Society of Children's Book Writers and Illustrators for the Work-in-Progress Grant, which helped make this book possible. Thanks to the talented writers who read early drafts of this book: Catherine Stine, Maggie Powers, Carolyn MacCullough, Melinda Howard, Tara Morris, and Jil Picariello. Special thanks to my sparkling agent, Kathleen Anderson, and my shimmering editor, Margaret Raymo, and the whole team at Houghton Mifflin. To the Westside YMCA Writer's Voice, for being such a great place to teach, with wonderful students who taught me as much as I tried to teach them. To my family, both nuclear and extended, deep gratitude for their tireless support. To Miles for making me laugh, and to Rich for making me happy.